"I told you—se...
enter my scheme of things!"

"You're my partner, Ben Ross." Sophie pulled away from Ben's innocent touch.
"You know this business of ours inside out, and we've got to cooperate . . . but for work only. I'm not in the market for any other form of casual involvement."

Ben didn't reply, but what he did do shocked Sophie to the core. Suddenly his arms trapped her, and his lips forced her head back in a kiss that left her both outraged and breathless.

"Nothing too casual about that, was there?" he asked harshly.

But Sophie didn't stop long enough to let his meaning penetrate. She turned and ran. Suddenly she realized that she had caused this change in this hitherto unchangeable man.

Books by Alison York

HARLEQUIN ROMANCE
2880—NO SAD SONG

That Dear Perfection

Alison York

Harlequin Books

TORONTO • NEW YORK • LONDON
AMSTERDAM • PARIS • SYDNEY • HAMBURG
STOCKHOLM • ATHENS • TOKYO • MILAN

Original hardcover edition published in 1988
by Mills & Boon Limited

ISBN 0-373-02970-5

Harlequin Romance first edition March 1989

CHAPTER ONE

'MISS PRYOR'S here, Mr Edwards.' The dark, very Welsh-looking receptionist stepped aside to let Sophie go past her into the solicitor's office.

Gareth Edwards stood to greet her and came forward, hand outstretched, his serious face breaking into a smile.

'Welcome to Abergavenny, Miss Pryor.'

People usually smiled at Sophie. She was a slender, finely built girl, small enough at the age of twenty-one still to be able to get away with modelling teenage fashion, and to be glad that her connections with the rag trade meant she was spared problems with off-the-peg clothes. Today she was wearing a honey-coloured silk jersey Gina Fratini dress that stood up to long journeys with amazing good temper, and this, combined with the shining warm gold of her hair, seemed to bring an invasion of sunshine into the sombre office.

'How was the journey?' the solicitor asked.

'Surprisingly quick. I left London far too early—but that didn't matter. I've been looking round the castle and the town.'

'Not a bad little place.'

'No, indeed. It's all so different from how I'd imagined it. Wales, I mean.'

Different from the way Margo, who didn't like to be called Mother, had represented it. Margo had only spoken disparagingly of the Wales spoiled by

man, of the rows of inadequate houses built by uncaring bosses, and of the slagheaps that dominated
them. Margo had not talked of purple-black soaring
mountains and lush green valleys with rivers
foaming and cascading through them. Margo, as
was her habit, had distorted the facts.

'Do sit down, Miss Pryor,' Gareth Edwards was
saying. 'I'm sorry to have insisted on your coming
all this way, but your uncle's estate is rather more
complicated than most. Mr Curtis's provisions
really do call for a meeting of the two main beneficiaries before matters can be settled. Now, shall
we have some coffee while we wait for Mr Ross to
get here?'

'That would be lovely. I'm afraid I must ask who
this Mr Ross is,' Sophie said. 'I'm sorry to be so
ill-informed, but I only knew Uncle Charles through
letters. We never actually met.'

'Ben Ross took over a directorship when your
uncle retired from active involvement in Country
Connection—the perfume factory?—but you know
about that, of course,' he added as Sophie nodded.
'For the past two years he's been Managing
Director. I think there was a close friendship between the two men—more than a mere working
relationship.'

'So things will go on pretty much as before at
the factory? That's got to be good for the business,
hasn't it?'

The solicitor hesitated for the briefest fraction of
a second, then said, 'We shall have a clearer picture
of that when Mr Ross arrives. Excuse me one
moment.' He spoke into the intercom and ordered

coffee, and when he again looked at Sophie it was to see a worried expression on her face.

'Mr Edwards, I feel awful about being here. I mean, I didn't even know that Uncle Charles had died until I got your letter. Maybe my mother was told, but I haven't seen her for weeks.' She pulled a wry, apologetic face. 'We're not the closest of families, as you've probably gathered. You see, my father—Uncle Charles's younger brother—died before I was born, and since then my mother has remarried twice, not very successfully. Perhaps my uncle disapproved—I really don't know. But we had no social contact with him. He paid for my education, and very generously, presumably for his brother's sake. But he never came to see us or asked us to go and see him. So I really feel that all I've done is take from him, and now I'm summoned after his death to act like a kind of—of vulture.'

With one hand plucking nervously at the fine gold bracelet on her wrist, and her hazel eyes clouded with worry, Sophie looked the very opposite of a vulture. Mr Edwards smiled kindly at her.

'My dear, you're here because your uncle wished it to be so. Of his own free will he has involved you in his estate, and there's no need whatsoever for you to feel as you do. These occasions are never exactly easy; they can be snarled up in feelings of all kinds ranging from sadness to greed. You have just shown me that you have no truck with the latter, so let's just treat this as a business meeting carefully planned in advance by Mr Curtis and conducted in the dignified, thoughtful way he would have wanted.'

There was a tap on the door and the girl who had admitted Sophie came in with a tray.

'Ah, thank you, Sandra,' Mr Edwards said. 'Perhaps if you put the tray near Miss Pryor she'll pour for us.'

Sophie was glad of something practical to busy herself with. Before the business of cream and sugar was sorted out, and the generous slices of buttered, fruity Bara Brith offered and accepted, the intercom buzzed and the receptionist's voice sounded clearly in the room.

'Mr Edwards, Mr Ross's secretary has just phoned. There's trouble on one of the production lines at the factory and Mr Ross has to stay until it's sorted out. He's very sorry. He should be able to come along this afternoon if that's convenient, but he daren't say any sooner than four-thirty.'

'Oh dear—can you possibly stay on until then, Miss Pryor?'

Sophie, wishing that the day didn't have to drag out in such a way, indicated that she could.

'Confirm that, then, Sandra. Thank you.' He looked at Sophie. 'How very unfortunate... and I have a lunch appointment which I can't possibly cancel, much though I would like to.'

'Don't worry, I can pass the time quite easily,' Sophie told him.

'I can at least recommend somewhere pleasant for you to eat. There's a town plan here.' He marked two or three places, then passed the plan to her, saying, 'Actually, this delay may turn out to be quite a good thing, Miss Pryor. I told you, I think, that your uncle's estate is rather more complicated than usual, and for that reason an hour or two to think over the implications of the bequest will be no bad thing. There's also a letter to you from your uncle—entirely private, its contents known neither to me nor to anyone else. This too may have some bearing on your decision.'

'I don't quite understand,' said Sophie. 'What do you mean by "decision"?'

'Let me pick out the clause that affects you most. That will be enough for you to think about at the moment.' Mr Edwards took the will from a folder on his desk, turned the pages until he found what he wanted, then, keeping his head discreetly lowered, he read to her.

' "Clause 2A: I bequeath joint ownership of the perfume manufacturing company known as Country Connection in Llangellert, South Wales, to Sophie Catherine Pryor of 105 Burbrook Road South, Battersea, London…and to Benedict James Ross, Managing Director of Country Connection, Llangellert. This bequest——" ' the solicitor's voice slowed significantly ' "—is conditional upon the willingness of both beneficiaries to guarantee active involvement in the running of the factory for a period no shorter than two years following my death." '

Mr Edwards paused, and looked at Sophie, who gazed blankly back at him as though petrified. She had expected some minor financial bequest, not this colossal offering of what amounted to an entirely new existence.

'But how could I do that? My life is in London. My future's worked out. May I see it?' she asked, and when Mr Edwards passed a copy of the will to her, she read through the words for herself. There they were, in black and white...no figment of the imagination.

'You see now why it was important for you to be here to meet Mr Ross so that you can talk through everything involved,' Mr Edwards said gently.

Sophie was reading the words again as though they could miraculously change into something more acceptable. '...conditional upon the willingness of both beneficiaries to guarantee...' She looked up. 'What happens if one of us can't...won't...?'

Mr Edwards helped her out sympathetically. 'Clause 2B explains what is to be done in that eventuality.'

Sophie read on. '"Should one or both of the beneficiaries fail to meet the conditions laid down in Clause 2A, the aforementioned company Country Connection will be sold to a prospective purchaser, details of whose offer are deposited with my accountants, Rymand and Napier, at their Monmouth office. Proceeds of the sale, together with that of other properties listed in Clause 3A and B, will be apportioned as follows between the aforementioned beneficiaries and the listed charities:——"'

Sophie stopped reading. There was an alternative. She couldn't take in any more right now.

Mr Edwards was taking a long white envelope from the file. 'What I suggest now is that you go away and have a quiet, serious think about this. Read your letter, mull it all over before you meet Mr Ross this afternoon.' He looked keenly at her. 'You'll be all right?'

Sophie managed a smile. 'I'll be fine. Stunned, but surviving.'

Mr Edwards thought she had hit the nail on the head. She was not as fragile as she looked, this small blonde girl with the firm chin and the eyes that expressed so much.

'That's the spirit! So I'll see you at four-thirty,' he said, rising.

Sophie slipped the letter in her shoulder bag and kept the town plan in her hand. She felt she was in a dream. 'Yes. Thank you, Mr Edwards.'

She couldn't face a big, solitary lunch in a public place, she decided quickly. A sandwich and somewhere private to read Uncle Charles's letter was what she needed.

A health food shop provided a couple of appetising salad rolls, and the back of the town plan suggested several walks that would take her away from everyone. She went back to the car first to change her high heels for her flat driving shoes, and to pick up a sweater.

All the walks involved mountains. She discounted Holy Mountain and the Sugar Loaf as being either too high or too far, and chose Little Skirrid, deciding she had big enough mental mountains to climb without tackling huge real ones. Then she made her way with determination to the footbridge near the station where the walk began.

A working partner in a business she knew nothing about . . . that was what Uncle Charles was trying to make her. In fact, now that she knew his intentions, the pattern of her life became much more clear, and she saw that this was what he had been planning for her from his position of remote control all along. This was where the insistence on maths coaching in her 'O' level year had been leading. This was why there had been so many protests when she wrote to thank him but politely decline his offer to subsidise a period of further education after Sixth Form, telling him that she had decided to try to make a career for herself in modelling.

Sophie had always wondered why on earth he had concerned himself so much with the education of a niece he seemed to have no wish to meet. In some ways his concern had been a blessing. A stable boarding-school 'home' in term time had compensated for the chequered holidays during which Margo was far more concerned with her own stormy love life than with her daughter. But now it was obvious that it was the future of his business that Uncle Charles had been planning for. He wanted his only surviving relative to carry on nursing his 'baby'—Country Connection—and he had done his utmost to fit her for the task.

All through that first shaky year of modelling he had persistently sent details of Business Studies courses to Sophie. Modelling was precarious, the accompanying letters emphasised. Why not another string to her bow? Perhaps she would eventually run a business of her own. Why not prepare herself for that possibility?

At first Sophie had tossed the literature aside. But as the year progressed, her attitude changed and she read the brochures more carefully. She realised now that her modelling life would be shorter than the average—and the average was short enough. Age would stop her teenage work in a year or two, and her size banned her from other fields.

Her assignments had been rather too sparse for complacency too, and money was tight. If she did as Uncle Charles insisted, she could still go on with her fashion work—it would only mean skipping the occasional lecture. And life would be so much easier with a financial subsidy she could count on.

She appeased her conscience by working extremely hard during her two years' Business Studies course at the Polytechnic of the South Bank. The days she missed because of her fashion work she made up for by nights of study, and although she began by finding it hard going, there was no denying that now at the end of her two years she had found in herself an aptitude and liking for the world of finance and business that she would never have dreamed herself capable of. So much so, in fact, that she had been thinking of working towards setting up her own model agency, the logical outcome of her two interests.

Sophie fingered the long white envelope in her bag as she walked. And now she had this enormous situation to sort out before she could get back to the world she knew. She hoped Uncle Charles's letter would not be an emotional plea—it would be most unlike him if it were. Their correspondence had always been restrained and strictly down to business. She quickened her pace as she neared the top of Little Skirrid, and once there and settled in a little hollow overlooking the town and river, she slipped a finger inside the flap of the envelope and tore it open.

'My dear Sophie,' the letter began, 'When you read this, the promise that has bound me since you were born will no longer be binding. I am free to tell you—and if there were an easy way of doing this I would take it, I assure you—that I have the right now as I never had in my lifetime to address you as "my dear daughter".'

Sophie's mind jolted at the words. What was he saying? This had got to be a mistake—his mind must have been deranged. Or—— Who had written this thing? She turned to the bottom of the second page and saw the signature . . . Charles Curtis . . . so there was no doubt that her uncle had written the letter. But *Adam* Curtis was her father. Margo had told her so, and surely Margo was the one to know.

A little questioning worm was working away in her mind, though. Margo had also fobbed off all Sophie's questions about her father with the impatient words, 'Don't keep digging over the past, child. Bother yourself about the living, not the dead.' And Margo, who was unbelievably cavalier about life's courtesies, had always insisted that thank-you letters to Charles Curtis were written promptly . . . Sophie suddenly felt a huge question mark opening in her life as her whole past history seemed to shimmer and move and threaten to rearrange itself in new and alarming patterns. Apprehensively she went back to the letter.

'It is for your mother to explain if she chooses why she made me swear never to attempt to see you, never to disclose our true relationship, before she would allow even the remote contact I have had with you. All I can do now is tell you that I should have been proud to own you as my daughter. That I could not do so was not my wish, Sophie, it was my sorrow. I hope you will believe that.

'I have tried through the only means within my power to ensure that your education made up for the uncertainties of your home background. I loved your mother against all the dictates of my own upbringing and nature, but even while I loved her, I knew her for the frailties she exhibits. From the photographs I persuaded each of your schools to send me, I saw that you were not like her, and this made me urge a course of study you were not at first willing to follow.

'By now you will know that I am putting before you yet another path that is not of your own choice. I beg of you to follow it a little way, Sophie. Test yourself against its challenge. You will not find the journey without its rewards.

'Nor will the community at Llangellert. The factory has brought work to an area that badly needed it, where unemployment shadowed so many lives. If Country Connection is sold, who knows what the next owner, who already, no doubt, has suitable plant for the continued manufacture of our small range in a more accessible part of the country, will do? The village's future, as well as your own, is in your hands. I realise that in telling you this I am putting what you may feel to be unfair pressure on you, but I believe my reasons, both personal and public, for this are valid ones.

'I am asking much of you. Perhaps the greatest thing I ask is that you may find it possible to understand and forgive the man who only now can declare himself your loving father,

'Charles Curtis.'

Sophie read the letter with painful slowness, going over each paragraph time and time again, her initial refusal to believe slowly forced to change into acceptance of the sincerity and truth that ran through Charles Curtis's words.

But why? The cry rang out inside her. Why had such a deception been perpetrated in her life? Why had she been prevented from knowing the father she had so often wished she had—until it was too late? What could Margo's motives have been?

Sophie sat on, like a figure in stone, the only movement that of soft strands of her hair stirring in the breeze. The letter lay in her lap, her fingers still tensely clutching it, and her eyes saw nothing of the panorama before them. Birds hopped close enough to plunder the picnic rolls that lay forgotten by her side.

Her past was in confusion. The course her future was to take must be decided before she summoned up her shattered resources and faced the solicitor to give him her decision. She would not tell him—would tell no one—what the letter contained. Such new, painful knowledge must be carried inside her until she understood it fully herself and could believe it in her heart as she was already compelled to do in her mind.

The receptionist was looking out for her when Sophie returned, five minutes late, to the solicitor's office. Time seemed to have entered another dimension, but the inbred habit of good grooming had prevailed and before coming back Sophie had once again slipped on her dainty shoes and restored her make-up. She had looked at her face in the cloakroom mirror, seeing it as that of a stranger. Her looks had nothing to do with Margo's dark elegance... so they must be derived from this unknown quantity, her father.

The serious conversation between Mr Edwards and the man with him ceased as Sophie was shown in.

'Ah, Miss Pryor,' said Mr Edwards. 'I hope you had a good lunch?'

Sophie had been so enmeshed in the problem of her own identity that she had forgotten someone else was involved in her decision, and the stranger's presence was a shock.

Her eyes met those of the man Mr Edwards was now introducing as Ben Ross, and before he could assume a mask of politeness she saw a flash of very different feeling in their dark, velvety brown depths.

He doesn't like me, Sophie thought. Why? He doesn't even know me.

'Miss Pryor,' he said, inclining his head briefly and taking her hand in a hard, enveloping grip. 'My sympathy on the death of your uncle—rather delayed, I'm afraid. I had hoped to be able to speak to you at the funeral.'

So there we have it, Sophie thought tiredly as she murmured her greeting and thanks. Weighed in the balance and found wanting. Well, Mr Ross, you know *nothing*, and it's going to stay that way. Think what you like, I've enough to worry about without any aggro from you!

'Have you put Mr Ross in the picture?' she asked, turning to the solicitor.

'I've gone over the clauses referring to Country Connection, as I did with you before lunch. What I propose now is to leave you together for a little while. I shall be in the next office should you want me to elucidate any points. I'm sure you'll feel more free to talk things over without a third party present. Then, if you're decided on your course of action, we'll take it from there.'

He smiled reassuringly at Sophie and left. Ben Ross, who had remained standing after greeting her, walked over to the window and looked down into the street in silence, his tall figure blocking the light and his broad shoulders stiff with hostility.

'Tell me,' he said, without looking at her, 'did you know the terms of your uncle's will, Miss Pryor?'

'No. I'm as—surprised by them as you are.' By them, and by so much more, she thought painfully, fighting down the surge of emotion that threatened. One thing at a time. She had to deal with one thing at a time.

He turned, hands thrust into the pockets of his suit, his jaw tightening. 'Hardly that, I think. You must have been expecting something. Its somewhat unexpected form is hardly in the same class as a total upheaval in the working environment of up-wards of fifty men and women.'

Sophie looked steadily at him. 'I think we'd better leave each other's reaction to our individual judgement, Mr Ross.' The look in his eyes spurred her on to add, 'I'm sure you'll find that whichever way the decision goes, there are compensations.'

'Do you think I care about myself?' Now his anger was open and sparking between them. 'I have no need of *compensations*, Miss Pryor. I've worked for the top chemical manufacturers in Europe, and I don't doubt I can do so again. My concern is for the company your uncle created, now destined on your whim to be swallowed up and digested by some big conglomerate or other. My concern is for the men and women who will lose their jobs in the process . . . and for the families who will suffer. No doubt they'll think as I do: to hell with compensations!'

Despite her emotional and physical tiredness, Sophie felt herself beginning to react to his hostility, but again she forced herself to speak calmly. 'Aren't you rather jumping the gun? Have I given you any indication which of the two options I intend taking?'

'Do you have to? Let's face it—in the seven years I've worked at Llangellert, the place has seen neither hide nor hair of you. With such a one hundred per cent absorbing life in London, and now the chance of a sizeable lump sum to keep the merry-go-round turning, your decision doesn't call for much guesswork.' He raised his hands and ran them through his dark, springy hair. 'I'm sorry, I shouldn't be speaking to you like this. But my strong feelings about Llangellert run away with me.'

He didn't look sorry. Sophie studied his lowering face for a moment as he looked down into the street again.

'So it would definitely be your choice, in spite of the condition attached, to go on running the factory?'

'What's the point of talking about my choice?' He didn't even do her the courtesy of looking at her. Sophie, tired of the verbal sparring he seemed determined to indulge in, went over to the door and spoke to the receptionist.

'Sandra, would you ask Mr Edwards to come back, please.'

They waited in a charged silence until the solicitor was behind his desk again. Mr Edwards eyed them circumspectly.

'Have you reached a decision?'

It was Sophie who answered. 'It seems that we're both agreed that Clause 2 of my uncle's will should be implemented.'

'Mr Ross?' The solicitor looked interrogatively at the man who was now staring disbelievingly at Sophie.

'Are you serious?' he asked.

Sophie smothered a sigh. 'Mr Ross, I see no reason to discuss this business with anything but seriousness.'

His dark eyes went on boring into hers. 'You've thought it through? Two years in the heart of Wales? That's what it means.'

'I've had the past four or five hours to think about it. I know exactly what it means, and I know

what I'm doing.' She turned back to Mr Edwards.
'I really would be grateful if we could get through
anything else that has to be dealt with as quickly
as possible. I had a very early start this morning,
I've got a long drive ahead of me—and another
busy day tomorrow.'

Mr Edwards nodded. 'You're in agreement, I take
it, Mr Ross?'

'I am. It's what Mr Curtis would have wanted,
but——' He broke off, then shrugged and said,
'Oh, leave it at that. This isn't the time to say more.'

'Then I think you'll find the rest of the will self-
explanatory, Miss Pryor. There's a property in
France which now remains on the company's
books, and the house in Llangellert which will be
put at your disposal. This is your copy: study it at
your leisure and come back to me with any queries.
All that's essential now is for you to sign this
agreement before two witnesses, which I'll arrange
at once.'

The rest of the meeting passed in a daze for
Sophie. She had made her decision, but she was
scared of it, and she was glad when she could take
her leave and go out into the street again where
shops were closing and people hurrying home.

A feeling of sudden faintness surprised her, and
she reached out to the nearest wall and stood with
lowered head fighting away the threatening
blackness.

'Are you all right? No—obviously not.' A firm
arm went round her and eased her down on to a
windowsill, then a hand on the back of her head
pushed it down towards her knees.

Him! Sophie thought, recognising Ben Ross's deep voice through the waves of dizziness, then she was forced to concentrate on hanging on to consciousness.

'Better now,' she said weakly after a few moments, wondering if she could trust herself to stand.

'*Did* you eat at lunchtime?' the no-nonsense voice asked. Then, at the slight shake of her head, 'I thought not. And you were about to put yourself and who knows else at risk on the M4. Hardly sensible. If you can make it across the road we'll get some food inside you.'

His hand gripped her upper arm, steadying her as she rose and supporting her across the road and into a pub.

When he had settled her at a table in the deserted bar, he went across and rapped on the counter until someone came through from the back. Sophie watched, resenting the situation but knowing it made sense to have her blood sugar restored to a working level. He was actually *charming* the landlord—who had begun by protesting that food was not on offer in the evenings—into heating up some of lunchtime's home-made soup and making a chicken sandwich.

His face as he spoke to the man looked completely different. There was warmth there now as well as strength, transforming the disapproving line of the mouth and the hostility she had seen in the dark eyes, making him look quite human. Big men should always cultivate kindness, she thought, her eyes going from the tamed anarchy of Ben Ross's dark hair and wandering down the broad back and long legs. Without kindness they constituted too much of a threat, especially to someone of her diminutive size.

He came across with a tray and put it in front of her. 'Get this inside you. And no nonsense about being on a diet. You look as though you don't eat enough to keep a sparrow going.'

Sophie thanked him. 'I have a perfectly normal appetite,' she added. 'It's just that today hasn't exactly been a normal day.'

He sat in silence, letting her get on with the soup. When the bowl was empty, he said, 'At the risk of being repetitive, are you sure you know what you're doing?' He was taking a deep draft of his lager as she considered her reply, watching her over the rim of the tankard.

'I think I'm doing the right thing,' she said, calmly starting on the sandwiches when she had spoken.

'For the factory, maybe. But what about you? How are you going to fit in? What have you been doing up to now?'

Something made Sophie hold back the information that she had been doing a Business Studies course.

'Modelling—fashion modelling,' she told him, and looked up to see his disapproval flaring again.

'For the moment I can't quite see the useful connection between that and active involvement in perfume manufacture.'

'I don't remember Clause 2 saying anything about qualifications or standards,' she retorted.

His mouth twisted sardonically. 'From what I observed, Charles Curtis was a man who had to be content without expecting high standards from anyone.'

Sophie pushed away the plate on which one sandwich was left.

'I know you're determined to dislike me, Mr Ross, so I'll not linger. I just hope you'll be able to moderate your attitude by the time we have to work together. You speak from a position of ignorance. You know nothing about the family situation.'

'I know that Charles Curtis was a very generous—and a very lonely man.'

His words brought back what Charles had said in his letter about his inability to acknowledge her as his daughter. 'That I could not do so was not my wish, Sophie, it was my sorrow.', and her eyes pricked suddenly with the first tears since reading it.

He saw, and let her know that he had seen. 'It's too late for tears. All we can do from this moment on is make the best job we can of what he left us to do.'

Sophie swallowed hard. She would not let him see her cry.

'Thank you for the food,' she said. 'I'll be in touch through Mr Edwards.'

'You aren't sufficiently interested to come out and have a look at the factory before you go back, then?'

She looked at him in exasperation. 'I've had enough for today. The factory can keep a bit longer.'

'But if it were a question of swanning off to France to Les Meules—the flower farm near Grasse...bags of sunshine...the Med close by——' he expanded sarcastically, 'I imagine you'd feel rather more enthusiastic.'

'Right!' Sophie said defiantly. 'I could do with a holiday. I'll make sure I take advantage of the place. Goodbye, Mr Ross.'

She turned then and left him, walking with quick, angry steps towards the car park. She had had quite enough of the man for today. He was far from being the most important thing to emerge from Charles Curtis's will. Of incomparably greater moment was the question that filled her mind to the exclusion of all else, now: Who am I? And the person who had to answer that, side-step and dodge the issue however much she might try, was Margo.

CHAPTER TWO

THREE weeks later Sophie was steering her little Mini through the early morning traffic, heading back to Wales and looking her last on the streets of London for the time being. She would have to come back briefly to honour a modelling booking for the friend who had first introduced her to the work, but apart from that her ties with the capital had been easily severed.

Not so easy, though, had been her confrontation with Margo and its emotional consequences.

Margo's first instinct when brought face to face with the truth of her own past had been to put as much distance between herself and her daughter as possible, but Sophie had braced herself against the door of the smart Knightsbridge flat and refused either to leave or to allow Margo out until she received the explanation due to her.

Now she knew, and gradually, after a succession of dark days she preferred not to think about, she was coming round to living with the knowledge. It was so far from the past she had wanted to believe in. In that imagined past, Sophie had seen herself as the loved and wanted child of a romantic marriage that had ended tragically with the death of her father before she was born—a perfect marriage, that went some way to explaining Margo's inability to find satisfaction in any other relationship. How different was the reality that had eventually come pouring from her mother's lips!

One thing had been true: Margo's hatred of the place of her birth. Born into a mining family, and growing up when pit after pit was closing, she had determined at all costs to get away from the place whose decay she felt was stifling her. Then, as now, her behaviour was impulsive, over-dramatic, dangerous. It wasn't enough to leave, to head for London and get work there. Margo was going to leave with a lump sum to cushion her against anything life could fling at her... and Charles Curtis, for whom she worked, was going to provide it.

'I could always get any man to do what I wanted,' she told Sophie—with some truth, for Sophie had seen her at work on so many men, but never to so disastrous an effect as she had on Charles Curtis.

A shy, introverted bachelor, long resigned to the continuing of his bachelorhood, Charles was quickly bewitched by the beauty of the capricious young Margo, who seemed so unbelievably to be in love with him.

It had been pitifully easy to make him an unknowing accomplice in her scheme. Things only went wrong when, faced with the news that Margo was pregnant by him, instead of subsidising a discreet disappearance as she had counted on his doing, Charles offered—no, more than that, *urged* marriage.

The thought of years with this quiet, sober man who was so much her elder and obviously intent on spending the rest of his life reproaching himself for what he thought he had done to her was enough

to send Margo flying to London without the money
she had calculated on getting from him. It was as
her panic receded in the first precarious weeks that
she began to think that probably all was not lost.
If the man had been so taken with her as to want
to marry her, he surely would be equally driven to
want to support his child?

Margo, once embarked on the story, spared her
daughter no cruel detail.

'If he hadn't come across with maintenance and
more, and absolutely on my terms, you wouldn't
be here. So you owe the man a couple of years in
the wilderness, I suppose, Sophie.'

'And what do *you* owe?' Sophie retorted hotly.
'Don't you feel any concern about the games you
played with two lives—his and mine? Why couldn't
you have told me the truth—let me know him? Why
couldn't you just have dumped me on him, and got
on with your own life? You never wanted me in it.
It sounds as though he had far more feeling for me
than you ever had. All I was to you was a pawn—
an expendable pawn who just managed to survive
the game.'

'You didn't do badly out of it,' Margo said with
an impatient shrug. 'Don Pryor spoiled you
rotten—and you owe your name to him. You
weren't exactly entitled to any other man's,
remember.'

Sophie looked at her, speechless with disgust. It
was incredibly hard to believe that any woman could
behave as Margo had done—and speak so callously
about it.

'And you were my security,' Margo went on
brazenly. 'If things got too bad—bad enough to

make the thought of life with Charles bearable—
you were my return ticket.'

This woman is my mother, Sophie thought painfully. There's no getting away from that. Half of
me comes from her. Her greed, her cunning, her
callousness could flow through my veins if I let
them.

But I won't. Her face took on such a look of
determination that the man in the next car, who
had been planning on taking off ahead of her at
the lights where they were held up, thought better
of it and let the little Mini go first.

Sophie forced herself to concentrate on what lay
ahead. There had been an exchange of letters and
phone calls with Mr Edwards, and today she was
to pick up the keys to Carreg Plas, the house mentioned in Charles Curtis's will, as she passed
through Abergavenny.

It was a converted chapel, Mr Edwards had told
her, and the prospect of living in such a place both
intrigued and disconcerted her. Charles Curtis had
moved there when his old home had become too
big and rambling for him. Carreg Plas was in
Llangellert, not too far from the factory.

From Ben Ross there had been one brief com-
munication. He understood from the solicitor, he
wrote, that she would be settling in over the
weekend of July the sixteenth and seventeenth. He
would therefore look forward to seeing her at
Country Connection on Monday the eighteenth,
and would make sure that he was free to talk to her
and show her round the factory. It was a mere duty
politeness letter, but the fact that he could force

himself to be polite was an advance on the mood of their first meeting.

The keys collected, Sophie should have turned left past the Llangellert name sign at the side of the road up the lane to the house, but instead she found herself driving on and through the town, following the Crickhowell road a little way until she reached the Country Connection site. There she parked on the opposite side of the road to the factory, and sat looking across at the place that was now half hers.

The building overlooking the road was old and ivy-clad, its past use as some form of business no doubt the reason that Country Connection had been allowed planning permission in such a beautiful site. Set back from the road and screened by trees were more modern blocks constructed in the same, probably local stone. The dark green and gold sign, with its italic lettering, was a facsimile of the logo on the Country Connection packaging, and the sight of it made a thrill of nervous excitement go through Sophie. It was hers...her business!

Suddenly it was not enough to be an observer from across the road. She wanted to see more— and now, not on Monday.

Beyond the glass doors of the visitors' entrance the reception area was carpeted in the distinctive Country Connection dark green, the walls papered in gilt and cream stripes. At the desk a young, pleasant-looking girl with a musical Welsh voice seemed doubtful when Sophie asked for Mr Ross.

'He never sees anyone without an appointment.' Her eyes took in the single heavy plait of gold hair and the slim hips in the tight black jeans, then returned sympathetically to Sophie's face. 'Was it about the lab assistant's job? He might make an exception, if so.'

Sophie wished she had either thought harder before rushing in, or dressed the part more appropriately.

'If you could just tell him Miss Pryor's here, I don't think there'll be any problem.'

'Miss Pryor?' The girl flushed. 'You're not——? Oh, goodness! Do forgive me.' She hid her confusion over the switchboard, and in seconds Ben Ross's voice was crackling impatiently over the internal phone, heightening the blush in the receptionist's cheeks and doing nothing to convince Sophie that her confidence in being welcomed was well placed.

'Now? She's not due until Monday.'

'Yes—she's here in Reception right now,' the girl said, attempting a cover-up and knowing that she was not succeeding. 'Would you like someone to bring Miss Pryor across to the lab, Mr Ross?'

There was a very audible sigh. 'No, keep her there. I'll be over in a couple of minutes.'

The girl smiled hopefully at Sophie. 'Mr Ross won't be a moment. Would you like to sit down, Miss Pryor?' She indicated a comfortable leather settee next to a pedestal flower arrangement opposite the desk.

'I think that if there's an office prepared for me— as I'm sure there is—I'd prefer to go along there and wait.' Sophie had no desire to have anyone else witness what looked like being a frosty greeting.

The girl jumped to her feet. 'Oh, yes . . . it's Mr Curtis's old office. If you'd like to come this way I'll show you. I could introduce you to Mr Davies, the Sales Manager. His office is next to yours and he's in this morning.'

And have him share Ben Ross's impatience? 'I'll just wait, I think,' said Sophie.

The office she was shown into overlooked the road and the sweep of glorious countryside beyond it: it was a pleasant, panelled room carpeted in red with a big old kneehole desk over by the window.

On the wall behind the desk was a portrait in oils bearing a small brass plate that said 'Charles Curtis, Founder, Country Connection'. It was dated two years after Sophie's birth date.

She went over to it and stood looking into the serious, withdrawn-looking face with the thick silvery-fair hair that grew so similarly to her own from the high forehead.

'Well . . . I'm here,' she said softly, 'and only you and I know the truth. I'm going to *do* something with this gift of yours. I'll make this business grow if I can. I'll live up to what you wanted, even if you can't see it.'

There was a lump in her throat, and that was no state to be in with this quick-tempered Ross man on his way to speak to her. Sophie sat in the swivel chair and looked out of the window at the incredible view topped by the wild, high crests of the Brecon Beacons, at the moment gilded by sunshine but still awesome in their grandeur.

Steps were approaching along the corridor, and she stood quickly, looking towards the door.

The moment Ben Ross appeared, white lab coat flapping, square gold-rimmed glasses giving him an unexpectedly professorial look, she cut the ground from under his feet.

'Don't say it. I know I shouldn't have given way to the impulse to come in today when it was all arranged for Monday, but I stopped to look at the factory and I just couldn't wait. I really didn't mean to be here at all.'

He looked her up and down, a slight expression of amusement flickering over his face. 'I believe you. That outfit has its undoubted charms, but it could hardly be said to be the latest in office chic.' He took off his glasses and tucked them in the top pocket of his white coat, then took her hand in his strong, warm grip. 'Well...welcome to Llangellert, since you're here. As you see, I happen to be on site this morning, and there are no appointments, so there's no great harm done. I take it you'd like to see round the place today... meet a few people?'

'If that's really not too inconvenient?' Encouraged by his not unfriendly attitude, she went on, 'Actually, since we're talking of clothes, I'm a little surprised by this.' She flipped the lapel of his lab coat. 'Don't tell me the average Managing Director goes around in protective clothing?'

'I'm first and foremost a chemist.' His dark eyes challenged her. 'And here at Country Connection we have no easy riders. No one sits around in an office playing boss. It's not that kind of set-up.'

'Good,' Sophie said calmly, her hazel eyes as firm as his. 'If it were, it wouldn't suit me. I intend *doing*, not keeping out of the way marking time.'

'Doing what, that's the question, isn't it, though?' He went on staring at her, his dark brow furrowed for a moment, then he turned briskly. 'Let's leave that until Monday. We'll start with the warehouses. You're going to be cold—some of them are temperature-controlled. Do you want me to get a lab coat for you? It would add a layer.'

'No, I'll be all right. I'm very warm-blooded.'

'*Are* you?' The slight emphasis on the 'are' gave the harmless response an inflection that had Sophie glancing quickly at him, but Ben Ross was striding out along the corridor, looking straight ahead.

'Ask Bron to deal with all my calls, Caitlin,' he told the girl on the desk as they passed. 'I'll be tied up for an hour or so.'

The first warehouse was enough to convince Sophie of how much she had to learn.

'I was expecting to see masses of flower petals,' she said, confronted by ranks of metal containers and drums.

'No. That part of the work is done for us. The business of extracting essential oils is a complicated one—and the timing is all-important. Take jasmine, for instance: the flowers have to be picked daily in the early hours, and processed at once to extract the best from them. When you consider that we use products from all over the world that are equally dependent on speedy processing, you'll understand why that part of the manufacture has to be done in the country of origin.' He touched a container marked 'ROSE ABSOLUTE'. 'This comes from Bulgaria—their roses are unequalled.' He walked along the rows, Sophie following him, fascinated. 'Sandalwood and vetivert from India. Ylang-ylang from Madagascar. Oak moss from Yugoslavia. Patchouli from the East Indies.' He stopped and looked down at Sophie. 'So you could say that we have the whole world in essence here. There are around four thousand materials available, two hundred in most frequent use.'

'It's a very romantic business, isn't it?'

'Do you think so? Earthy too. We use some pretty fundamental materials as well. This, for instance—civet. And this—musk. They come from fairly unsavoury animal glands. And there's ambergris from the sperm whale.'

'How on earth did anyone ever discover that such things could be used in perfume?' Sophie said wonderingly.

'The origins of their use go too far back for anyone to know about in detail. Do you know that a piece of musk the size of a pinhead can perfume a whole room for weeks? The early Arab mosques had it mixed in their mortar so that they gave off perfume in the blazing sun.'

'I shall enjoy learning about all that,' Sophie said confidently, quickening her step to keep up with him as they moved on to the product warehouse.

'"All that" isn't what occupies us to any great extent here, I'm afraid. Here the emphasis has to be rather more on the laws of supply and demand, and on rows of tedious figures.' The genuine involvement in the background of his work that she had sensed and responded to was switched off, and he was once again the brisk, factual guide as they went into the product warehouse.

'You don't see Country Connection in the average chemist's, so where *is* the market?' Sophie asked, looking at the cellophane-wrapped sixes of attractive boxes. There were lines she hadn't known about—pretty drawer liners, pomanders, liquid soaps... whole ranges that were new.

'Specialising in single florals as we do, we tend to have the one-off market. Craft shops, country houses opening to the public, health food shops—now *that's* a rapidly growing outlet. Some of the big stores are beginning to feature us as a shop within a shop. We've just negotiated one in an Oxford Street department store—quite a bit of kudos in that.'

He stopped as they reached the other end of the warehouse and prepared to cross over to the next block.

'Are you sure you don't want a lab coat?' His eyes lingered for a moment on the white silk shirt she was wearing, and the curves over which it gleamed.

'I'm fine. We've finished with the cold area now, haven't we?'

He shrugged. 'On your own head be it, then.' At that moment the precise meaning of his rather odd words escaped Sophie, but she was soon to find out.

As he held open the door of the bottling area, someone crossing the courtyard attracted his attention for a moment and he indicated that Sophie should wait inside for him.

She found herself on a small open landing at the top of a short flight of steps down to the floor. The room was noisy, but she gradually realised that a percentage of the noise was in response to her presence. The men were tapping on the machinery with whatever lay to hand, grinning up at her as the metallic chorus grew to deafening proportions.

Sophie's cheeks grew hot as she stood there on her exposed perch. She didn't know where to look. Her jeans felt like a much too tight second skin, and her shirt seemed to cling with an excess of static. She would have given anything for the lab coat that fiend of a Ben Ross had so obliquely offered. He had known damned well that this was going to happen.

After what was probably only seconds, but seconds that felt like hours, Ben Ross pushed open the door and joined her, smiling sardonically at her obvious embarrassment.

'Pity you didn't accept my offer...' he said as the noise died down. 'That's a traditional visitors' reception here—especially when they look like you!'

'You might have warned me,' Sophie said shortly, but she held her head high as she followed him down the stairs. She might look like a schoolgirl, she might be small enough to be overlooked—but let no one here consider her anything other than a force to be reckoned with. In the meantime, they'd had their joke and enjoyed it. She wouldn't hold it against anyone—not even the giant she was now following.

She listened carefully to Ben Ross's explanation of the different procedures, her eyes shrewdly taking everything in as they went through the different areas from production through bottling to packaging and labelling.

'You'll have noticed that the blended perfume doesn't go straight through to bottling,' Ben Ross remarked. 'There's an essential period for maturing in the dark at ten degrees.'

'I also noticed,' Sophie said thoughtfully, 'that there was a lot of machinery standing idle. Does that mean that you're not producing to capacity?'

'It means we don't need to process that particular product at the moment.'

'But surely,' she persisted, 'the more you make, the more you put on sale...the more you sell. It seems very wasteful to have all that costly plant standing idle. It doesn't make sense.'

'Nor does over-production make sense. Our products have to be fresh—perfume deteriorates with age. We tread a very tight path between supply and demand.'

'So how about increasing the demand? I still see no point in idle machines and presumably idle men.'

'Ah, but there you presume wrongly. Our staff—all the work force, in fact—train in every process. Each employee can work in every area: does so, in fact, and the variety is popular. So the people you saw on the working production lines today also work on the idle ones when necessary.'

'And the demand? Increasing it, I mean?' Sophie was nothing if not persistent.

'I explained, I thought, that we have a restricted line of single florals and a far from mass market.'

Sophie picked at her shirt cuff thoughtfully. 'There must be something that can be done to improve the situation. I'm sure there must.'

His dark eyes looked coldly down at her as they paused in the courtyard. 'Then isn't it sad that we poor souls who've worked our way through the business for years have failed so lamentably to spot this flaw which you, in your wisdom, detect after mere minutes in the factory? Perhaps we've been waiting for this moment, and you're come among us to bring the light.'

'When you bite, you bite hard, don't you?' Sophie said drily.

'I suppose I've been hoping that you'd turn out to be more of an angel than the other kind—the kind that rushes in. Now I'm not so sure.'

'All right. I concede that that was a snap comment, and I've a lot to learn before I can be sure of making a valid one. I intend learning.'

'Good. I'm glad to hear you're aware of the necessity.'

'But——' she went on, 'I also intend questioning. If this place is half mine—as we both know it is—then I shall want to know it's as good as it can be.'

'You prove to me that an ex-model can achieve what a group of professionals can't, and I'll stand corrected.'

'I might do just that,' said Sophie, warm with the satisfaction of knowing that she had kept her business training to herself. It would be very rewarding to see this know-all who was so sure of himself find out that he was in partnership with rather more than a frivolous clothes-horse.

She refused his offer to take her in to meet more of the team, saying that she was content to wait until Monday for all that, but she was not to get away so easily. When Ben Ross saw the Mini loaded to the roof with all her worldly goods, he insisted, much against her wishes, on going to Carreg Plas with her to help her unload.

'You can tail me and save getting lost,' he said, dismissing her protest. 'And don't be so foolish as to resent offers of help. I'm built for the job; you obviously aren't.'

'I'm tougher than you think,' said Sophie, and repeated crossly to herself, 'Much tougher!' when she had slammed the driving door between herself and him. Damn it, she might not be as well clued up on Country Connection as he was—*yet*—but she could at least tote a few parcels around. If this was a preview of how he intended ordering her around at the factory, there were hard times coming for both of them!

He drove a grey Rover—a heavy car for a heavy-handed man, she thought as she followed him feeling like a toy dog in the Mini, back through Llangellert and then along winding lanes until eventually he stopped in front of what was unmistakably Carreg Plas.

Sophie had just time enough to notice the arched windows in the dark red brick walls of the tiny ex-chapel, and to see that a cottage next to it had been cleverly extended sideways to link up and make a larger house out of the two buildings. Then Ben Ross was holding open the white gates and signalling that she should drive in.

'Pull in down the side as far as you can,' he ordered, stooping to speak through the window. 'Give me the keys and I'll open the french window at the back to let you in. It'll be easier to unload that way.'

Sophie pretended not to hear. She had every intention of letting herself into the house, however much he might issue his orders. She came back to the big chapel door and stood looking at the bunch of keys. None looked to match the oversized keyhole.

'Try the cottage door,' Ben Ross said with exaggerated patience. 'If you had the key to that one, there'd be no mistaking it.' He followed her round and managed to spoil her first impressions of the house simply by being there. Sophie would have liked to be free to rush around seeing everything for herself. Instead she had to control her curiosity and be satisfied with a perfunctory glance at the hall and kitchen as they went through to the main room in the ground floor of what she must stop thinking of as the chapel.

No wonder there had been no key to the huge door! It was obviously only retained as an external feature, and inside the whole wall around the arched windows was faced with warm gold stone with niches for a collection of antique glass. The rest of the walls were white, and a gold carpet and long velvet curtains were a pleasant foil to dark antique tables and big, comfortable chairs and sofa with loose covers in muted autumn colours.

'The master bedroom is up there.' Ben Ross pointed to a glass wall overhead at the back of the room, reached by an open flight of stairs against the wall. 'It was the balcony once before the conversion. There's a bathroom opening off. You'll find a couple of guest rooms and another bathroom over the kitchen, and the stairs to those go from the hall where we came in.' He was unfastening the french windows as he spoke. 'Now, if I bring everything in from the car and put it in here, you can take it where you like. Right?'

You mean you're giving me a choice? Sophie thought sarcastically, but she managed a cool, 'Thanks very much.'

The first box he brought in was full of kitchen equipment, so that gave her the chance of a good look around there. Warm cork tiles on the floor, well polished . . . rough brick walls, white-painted, and mellow wood units. Someone had put a bowl of summer flowers on the round dining table in the alcove overlooking the garden.

She ran up to look at the bedrooms, and found a door through on to the landing at the top of the stairs in the main room. Her bedroom was surprisingly feminine and mainly white, the only touch of colour being the shimmer of pale lemon silk curtains at the huge plate glass window over the sitting-room. The window at the back showed a panorama of wooded hills with here and there the white, whipped water of mountain streams, and the high Beacons beyond.

Ben Ross's voice made her jump. He came into the room with an armful of dresses on hangers. 'I thought I might as well bring these straight up. This room has been redecorated, by the way. It was pretty sombre . . . your uncle's taste.' He dropped the clothes on the bed. 'Nearly done now. By the time you've hung this lot up I'll have the last of the stuff out of the car.' He was off down again before Sophie could answer. She shrugged philosophically and opened up the wardrobe; there would be time enough to spar for position later.

When she had finished, she went over to the huge glass wall and looked down into the sitting room out of casual interest, but what she saw sharpened her attention dramatically.

Ben Ross, with his back towards her, was taking something from a drawer in the storage unit under the stairs, and putting it in his pocket.

Quickly Sophie went out of the bedroom and ran down. He turned, not at all discomfited.

'I was just about to suggest a welcome drink.' He opened the doors of a cupboard well stocked with assorted bottles and glasses.

'You seem to know your way around,' Sophie remarked.

'So will you, in no time at all. It's an easy house to get used to. What will you have?'

All right, Sophie thought. Two can play that cool-as-a-cucumber game!

'What I'd really like,' she said calmly, though her heart had quickened, 'is the answer to a question. Which of Charles Curtis's papers were interesting enough for you to put them in your pocket to take away just now?'

His expression chilled, but the hold of the dark eyes on hers did not waver. He put a hand in his jacket pocket and withdrew a letter, clearly addressed to B. Ross, Carreg Plas, Beacon Road, Llangellert.

'There really is no need, but perhaps I should offer you the chance to check my other pockets?' he said coldly. 'The reason this was here, and the reason I know this house so well, is that when your uncle was too weak to be left alone at night I moved in and slept here for as long as he needed me. It was no hardship—I was in a rented house. I lived here for almost three months. So it's hardly surprising and not at all criminal that one or two things were overlooked.' He closed the cupboard doors firmly.

Sophie felt dreadful. 'I'm sorry. I wish you'd just said.'

'I hardly like referring to that time to you—for obvious reasons—unless it's absolutely necessary.'

She floundered for words, and decided there were none that would make the situation any better. 'Let's have a drink and forget it, then.'

'Maybe the drink wasn't such a good idea after all. I'll get back to the factory.'

She followed him to the door, tonguetied with embarrassment.

'It makes me feel doubly bad to think you've had to move out of here for me, on top of everything,' she told him.

He stopped momentarily and looked at her, his craggy face cold and stern. 'Neither of us is doing anything *for the other*. I've been waiting for the house I now own to become empty for five years. The reason you're here at Carreg Plas, and that we're in this regrettable association at Country Connection, is that Charles saw fit to arrange it. It's as simple as that. We shall meet on Monday.'

Before she could even thank him for his help, he was gone. Sophie sank on to one of the kitchen chairs and slumped over the table, her head in her hands.

She had crashed in on him at the factory. She had annoyed him with her remarks about organisation there. And now she had implied that he was a thief when he appeared to be some kind of uncomfortable saint.

What an unfortunate, ominous beginning to what promised to be an ill-starred relationship!

CHAPTER THREE

THE WEEKEND slid by surprisingly quickly. Sophie spent a lot of time arranging her own personal possessions and getting to know the house and its contents. She felt something of an interloper, there were so many of Charles Curtis's private papers in every drawer and cupboard. Most of them were of little interest and she packed them away in boxes.

One very special find in the drawer of a little escritoire on Saturday afternoon caught her emotions very much on the raw, though. Every letter she had ever written to the man she had thought of as Uncle Charles was there, carefully kept. Sophie read through a few of them, seeing the impersonal, polite phrases with new eyes now that she knew they were the only link a man had had with his daughter. There was little comfort in them for her, and there must have been precious little for him. He had kept them, though...tied together with the kind of pink tape beloved of the legal profession.

She felt the need to get away from the house after that, and took off over the garden wall and up the hill behind the house, only coming back just in time to dash into Llangellert before closing time for a few last-minute groceries from the first supermarket she came across.

Each morning she awoke to the surprisingly varied bleating of sheep on the hill, and when it began to grow dark, twice she saw the powerful swoop of an owl across the sky, and heard the shrill, brief cry of its prey. London seemed continents— not just miles—away.

Monday morning was going to be something of a feat of endurance, largely of her own making, Sophie thought ruefully, but she got up early and told herself not to be stupid—Ben Ross was only a man!—then set about making herself look as equal to the task as possible.

She had washed the car on Sunday evening, and as she walked out to it and saw herself reflected in the Mini's gleaming panels, she thought that they were a very smart pair. Every inch the young executive, she thought, pausing before her reflection. She was wearing a chestnut-brown skirt, full at the hem but snug at the hip and waist, a crisp white shirt, and a black melton jacket. She had fixed her hair in a shining, intricate gold knot on top of her head to add height, and for the same reason she was wearing her highest black patent heels.

Caitlin on Reception was prepared for her this time with a 'Good morning, Miss Pryor,' and a secret, admiring survey of Sophie's clothes.

'Good morning, Caitlin. Had a good weekend?' Sophie asked, pausing at the desk.

'Average. Weekends in Llangellert aren't exactly wild!' the girl smiled. 'Mr Ross is tied up in the laboratory for a couple of hours, he said, but Mr Davies is in his office.'

'In that case, I'll introduce myself.'

Sophie went along the corridor and tapped on the door next to hers. There was the sound of busy typing from Ben Ross's office on the other side, she noticed, before a deep, pleasant voice called to her to come in.

Owen Davies was perhaps in his forties, with a thick thatch of prematurely grey hair over a young-looking face, and keen blue eyes that warmed appreciatively as Sophie introduced herself.

'There's a definite family resemblance, but you're decidedly the prettier one!' he said humorously, shaking Sophie's hand warmly. 'We were sorry to lose your uncle. He was a fine man, and Llangellert has much reason to be grateful to him. It's good that we shall still have a member of the family in the firm.'

Sophie thanked him. 'I feel a bit at a loss right now, but I hope I shall be useful eventually,' she told him, at once at ease with him. 'What I thought I'd do to begin with is get to know the place. Read the company records...spend some time on the floor watching what goes on... Then I may be able eventually to see where I'm going to fit in.'

He nodded. 'For the company records you'll have to see Ben—he has the files in his office now, but I'm sure they can be moved across to yours if you like. If you want to talk over the sales side, I've got this year's and last year's figures in here. And if you want to meet any of our customers, I'll let you have my schedule and you can come visiting with me any time you like.'

'I'll take you up on that later,' said Sophie. 'I think first of all, though, I've got to know more about what we do and how we do it. I'd like just to hang around watching and talking to people...get the feel of the place, you know. Would that be disapproved of?'

'Not at all. You'll need the right gear, though—
we're strict about protective clothing. Shall I fix
that for you?'

'If you would.'

He went through into his secretary's office and
gave the appropriate instructions. '—and one of the
daintier sizes,' Sophie heard him add. 'Take it along
to Miss Pryor's office for her, please, Maia.'

When he reappeared Sophie thanked him. 'And
now I'll get out of your way,' she said as she moved
to the door.

'If you really want to understand this place,' he
said as he came out into the corridor with her, 'get
Ben to talk to you about it. He knows the business
like the back of his hand. He should do, too—because he'd worked his way through every department on the factory floor before a word was
breathed to anyone that he'd been one of the top
chemists in Switzerland. He's got qualifications as
long as my arm, and he'd produced work that broke
staggering new ground in cosmetic allergy research
before he was twenty-five. All that behind him, and
yet he's given himself one hundred per cent to this
modest little factory in the heart of Wales. He's
been here seven years now. Mr Curtis thought the
world of him.'

And so did everyone else, apparently, Sophie
thought as she rather self-consciously donned the
white overall and headscarf waiting in her office,
at the same time calculating that Ben Ross must be
somewhere in his thirties now. As Owen Davies had
said, it was odd that he should be satisfied with this
place after his illustrious past . . . but he'd not done
badly out of it. He owned half of it now, which

was more than would have happened if he'd stayed on in Switzerland.

She pulled a face at her ghostly reflection in the window. So much for the young executive image! There wasn't much left of it now.

'Oh, well...' she said to herself, 'in at the deep end, Sophie. It's got to be done.'

This time there was no 'strangers' chorus' tapping on the machines, and Sophie found herself accepted as someone who belonged when she went into the first of the production units. The supervisors were eager to explain each process, and the workers glad to demonstrate, and she felt as the morning passed quickly that she was beginning to get a layman's picture of perfume manufacture.

She was being allowed to try a small part in the packaging operation when she suddenly realised that Ben Ross was standing watching her. Her momentary loss of concentration made a log-jam of bottles begin to pile up and topple alarmingly.

'Oh, heavens!' Sophie exclaimed, panicking helplessly, while the amused worker by her side stepped calmly forward and with hands that moved like lightning got the line moving correctly again.

'I'd like to drag you away for a few minutes,' said Ben Ross. At least he wasn't laughing at her.

'I should think it would be a welcome relief to the professionals. Thanks for sorting me out,' Sophie said with a warm smile to the woman whose job she had been attempting.

'We'll go over to the lab,' Ben Ross said as they made for the door. 'You didn't see that on Friday.'

With their last meeting recalled clearly by the mention of the day, Sophie turned to him impulsively as they came out into the courtyard.

'I want to apologise for Friday. It really was awful—one of the worst moments of my life!'

His dark eyes looked down at her. 'If there are none worse than that, you'll do well. Forget it. Water under the bridge. Much more important are two points I must make. The first is: don't go on the factory floor in shoes like that.' He pointed to her high heels. 'We have enough difficulty ensuring that the workers dress for safety without setting them a bad example ourselves. The second point affects morale rather than safety. Don't make yourself everybody's friend on the floor if you're going to go swanning off again and giving the whole thing up in no time at all. People are pleased to have you here as your uncle's representative, as you've probably gathered. I should hate to see them disappointed.'

Sophie stopped. 'Is that the kind of person you think I am?'

He gave a slight shrug. 'How do I know what kind of person you are? I haven't a lot to go on, have I? And what I have doesn't add up to make sense. An absentee niece... a London model, suddenly hamstrung by the terms of a will into playing factory proprietor. Anyone would have misgivings.'

'I'd rather you judged me by what you find out at first hand—and you haven't exactly given yourself the time to do that, have you?' she countered firmly. 'This is my first morning here. I don't want to hear talk about my giving up. Believe me, Mr Ross, I don't give up easily. I may not have expected to become involved in Country Connection, but perhaps I should remind you that I had the chance to "swan off" with a sizeable sum of money and let the factory go to pot—and I chose to come here. So here I'll stay for the next two years, in spite of all your Cassandra-like prophecies.' Her eyes narrowed determinedly. 'And probably more. So it would be as well if we could treat each other with a bit less prejudice, don't you think?'

For the first time there was the hint of a smile on his craggy face. 'You have spirit—I'll add that to the brief curriculum vitae. As a matter of fact——' he held the lab door open for her to go in '—I rather admired the way you tackled me about that letter when I thought about it. Far better than wondering and festering.'

Heaven be praised—a compliment! Sophie thought, then was spared the embarrassment of answering as her interest was captured by her surroundings.

'So this is where the creating's done,' she said, looking round at the pristine benches and equipment. 'Tell me about it.'

'How much do you know about perfume?' he asked.

'Which ones I like...and what I've seen here. So, not a lot.'

'Right.' He walked over to a seat in front of which were banked serried ranks of small bottles, looking like tiny organ pipes. 'These are the ingredients—but this isn't where the real creating's done. That job belongs to someone we call in the trade a "nose", because of his obvious talents; he works to our specifications to create the type of perfume we want and the kind of person we're aiming to sell to. He has so hyper-developed a sense of smell that he can distinguish not only the various ingredients of a perfume, but their exact country of origin. I have to rely on this.' He pointed to a piece of equipment against the wall. 'It's a spectrophotometer, and it can analyse exactly what ingredients and how much of them make up a particular perfume.'

'So if you don't do the original blending, what do you do here?'

'Various things. Make adjustments to the original recipe for one reason or another. Perhaps the top note—the first sensory impression—goes off too quickly. Maybe the middle note—that's the one that gives the fragrance its particular character—is not strong enough. Or it could be that the end note, the one that gives the fragrance its lasting power, isn't really effective enough. It's a very finicky business, but you don't need to worry your head about all that.'

'But I do!' Sophie said decisively. 'I want to know everything.'

'And in the shortest possible time, I suppose,' he said drily, then went on before she could protest. 'Here, come and look at this.' He led her into a small side room. 'This is one thing I've been exercising my detective powers on recently.' He showed her a roll of pretty lining paper, freesia-scented. 'We've had complaints about this one. It was losing scent far too quickly, or rather the perfume was changing, and not for the better. We couldn't isolate the fault at first. Lab tests on the ingredients were perfectly satisfactory. In the end it turned out that a change of one minor chemical in the manufacture of the original paper was responsible. It was reacting adversely with our ingredients. Simple when you know the answer.'

In spite of her protestations of fervent interest, Sophie found herself sidetracked into studying the change in Ben Ross when he spoke about his work. The aggression, the tendency to be critical, were plus points in this context, and she could see how he would persist in his pursuit of excellence with absolutely dogged determination.

She became aware that he had stopped speaking, and, unable to comment precisely on what he had been saying, she fell back on a safe, 'That's fascinating!'

As they came out of the little room, she saw little brass stands on a bench with strips of paper clipped to them.

'What are those?' she asked.

'I'll show you—test how good a "nose" you'd be.' He unscrewed three tiny phials and put a few drops from each on the absorbent strips on three separate stands. 'This is the same perfume at different stages of maturity. See if you can tell the difference.' He held the first stand to her nose and she sniffed obediently, then the second and third. 'Well?' he asked.

Sophie couldn't answer. Something extraordinary had happened. She had been far more aware of his hand, so close to her face, than of the perfume. His fingers were well manicured, long and tapering, and she could see the pulse in his wrist beating rhythmically, a tiny evidence of the strength in him. She had been seized by a ridiculous urge to lean forward and touch that fluttering life-point with her lips. How strange that she, who had seen enough of Margo's sexual capers to put her off any experimenting of her own, should suddenly in this unlikely spot and with this improbable man feel this disconcerting stirring of what she could only describe in novelettish terms as sheer animal desire. She could feel her telltale fair skin beginning to colour, and before Ben Ross could become aware of it too she turned aside with a little laugh.

'No good, I'm afraid. They all smell the same to me.'

'Oh, nonsense! Try again.'

Sophie did, but this time she held the stand herself and walked away a little, putting a prudent distance between them. Free from the absurd distraction of the first attempt, she was able to distinguish a difference, even if she couldn't be precise about it.

She kept a firm hold on herself for the rest of the time she was in the lab, and as she was leaving, her head bursting with information, she remembered the other range of facts she wanted to have a look at.

'Owen Davies said you had the company records in your office. Would it be possible to have them moved across to mine?'

He looked with quick suspicion at her. 'What on earth do you want that lot for?'

'It's not enough to look at the company as it is today. I want to see where it's come from ... how it's grown.'

'It would be much more relevant, surely, to think towards the future.'

Sophie felt a surge of impatience. 'If you don't want them moved, I can always crash in and out of your office to get what I want. It's all the same to me. I'm not embarking on any kind of power struggle, if that's what you're thinking.'

His burst of laughter was not flattering. 'Oh, take the things! Tell Bronwen to arrange for them to be moved. I resent change, that's all. I shall have to move my furniture around to fill the gap.'

'Thank you, Mr Ross,' Sophie said with exaggerated politeness. 'If you need help with the re-arranging, do call on me.'

'Miss Pryor——' he called after her. She turned and looked back at him. 'We're a simple bunch of people here, no airs and graces. You might as well cut out the "Mr Ross".'

Sophie's bright head inclined graciously, catching the sunlight.

'Thank you again, Mr Ross. That means change, too. But I'll try to get round to it.'

She had seen to the transferring of the records and was up to the end of Country Connection's second year when there was a tap on the door and Ben Ross walked in, his lab coat exchanged for the grey suit jacket that sat with the smoothness of superb tailoring on his broad shoulders.

'Time for lunch,' he said, 'or had you forgotten again?'

Sophie looked at her watch. 'Goodness! Is it as late as that? But you don't have to trundle me

around. I'm perfectly capable of finding somewhere for myself.'

'Not the best place, though. I thought I'd take
you to a favourite of mine, and point out one or
two others, plus the high spots of Llangellert. Just
a one-off trundle, I must emphasise—I don't have
time for social lunches very often. But I want to
talk to you. I've had an idea about what you could
do here. Come on, put this on.'

He took her jacket off the hanger and helped her
into it, while Sophie smothered the urge to tell him
she would get her own ideas in her own good time.

'So what's this plan of yours?' she asked when
she was settled in the Rover.

'Later, while we're eating. Now, there's an inn
just along here that specialises in jacket potatoes
with a range of about thirty different fillings.' He
drove her round town, pointing out the library and
post office and banks, and showing her the starting
points for some of the good local walks listed on
a leaflet he took from the glove box to give her.

The Fox and Grapes, where the mini-tour ended,
was lost in the lush green countryside on the banks
of the Usk. It was an old coaching inn with a huge
open fire, there no matter what the season, he told
her, and a particularly delicious line in home-made
flans and salads.

Sophie made her choice, then, while Ben got their
drinks, she went along to the cloakroom to tidy up
since she had been rushed away from the factory
without the chance to do so.

She was aware as she walked back to the table
in the window alcove that Ben was watching her
every step of the way, not casually, but intently.

'Well, will I do?' she asked as she sat down.

'Admirably. And that's where my idea comes in.'

Sophie picked up her knife and fork. 'Are you going to tell me about it now?'

'Why not? What qualities would you say were essential for a model?'

'That's a question, not an explanation.'

'I know. Just answer it. It *is* relevant.'

Sophie rested her knife and fork and thought a moment. 'Firstly personality, because looks are no good without it. Then something difficult to define...the ability to put yourself across, I suppose. And thirdly, of course, the size and shape and face that happens to be in fashion.'

He was looking pleased. 'The first two qualities are what I hoped you'd say.' His dark eyes raked her slowly from head to foot. 'We can take the looks for granted. Nobody wants to argue about that. And I know you can make out a good case for yourself against opposition—spoken or unspoken. All that seems to add up to the fact that you could be a useful asset on the public relations side for Country Connection. Know anything about it?'

Sophie managed to look calmly at him, despite the feeling that she was being well and truly patronised. 'I know what PR is. Roughly speaking, I suppose you mean that I could go on being a glorified model, only instead of "selling" clothes, I "sell" perfume.'

'Something like that. We've kept a fairly low profile so far. What you said on Friday about expanding the market made me think.' His eyes wandered slowly over her face again. 'You've got that rather special type of English look...fair hair, fair skin . . . and we make what most people think of as English flower products. It would seem to make sense for you to work along the lines of using your obvious talents.'

Sophie went on with the calming business of eating her lunch.

'But I may have other talents not yet discovered, mayn't I? And I was actually rather looking forward to a change of occupation.' She looked up at him, and her hazel eyes glinted challengingly. 'You don't like changes, though, do you? You prefer to keep your original impression of me and slot me into the firm somewhere where you feel I'll do the least harm.'

Ben leaned forward. 'Do you know that your eyes get decidedly more green-flecked when you're angry?'

'I'm not usually on the receiving end,' Sophie said tartly.

'And I'm a bit taken aback to find myself in that position. It was meant to be a helpful suggestion. You need a place in the firm. You can't go on floating around in a vacuum for ever, can you?'

'Like fall-out from Chernobyl? Is that how you see me?'

His face broke into a smile, the attractiveness of which she registered in spite of the circumstances.

'Hardly. You've got rather too well-defined a physical form for that. Let's change the subject now. Mull over the idea at your leisure—maybe you'll find it has something to recommend it, maybe not. I can't push it, can I? Now: tell me about yourself. Was it hard to leave London? Have you many family links there?'

'Only a mother who spends most of her time trying to forget she is—so no, hardly any family links at all. We see each other when it's necessary, and that's about it.'

'And what about any other . . . attractions?'

'Men? No, no one. I saw enough of the havoc my mother's hormonal impulses created in her life to be quite put off getting myself involved with anyone.' Sophie placed her knife and fork neatly side by side and gave him a bright smile. 'That was lovely. You did me a favour, introducing me to this place.'

Ben didn't respond. He was looking seriously at her. 'You paint a picture of a rather unnatural lifestyle.'

Sophie shrugged. 'What's natural? My mother's behaviour was natural enough, only too much so— and it doesn't seem to have brought her any lasting happiness. A bit of temporary gratification is the most she ever got out of a relationship. I certainly don't want to be like her—*ever*. Most people react against someone or something, don't they? The reagent in my case is more powerful than most, that's all.'

Unexpectedly he put a hand over hers as it rested on the table.

'You're far too young to be so cynical about life,' he said.

'I may not have many years notched up, but believe me I've plenty of experience,' she told him, then she looked up and met his eyes. 'And there's been no shortage of people trying to prove to me how wrong I am—with no success at all. In my own way, I'm perfectly happy.' She looked out of the window and at the same time withdrew her hand, hoping her words were enough to convince him that she wanted his sympathy no more than his attempt to organise her. 'Oh, look, it's pouring down!'

'That's something you'll get used to here. Why else do you think Wales is so green? I've got an umbrella in the car. I'll go and get it...unless you'd like anything more?'

'No, really. That was lovely. I shall certainly come again.'

Sophie stood in the porch while Ben dashed over to the car park for the umbrella, thinking that their conversation had taken a very unexpected turn. Ben Ross was not such a hard man as he had at first appeared, and that wasn't entirely an advantage. She hoped she wasn't going to be fighting him off, as she'd had to do with one or two others. She wanted her energies for the task in hand—and that wasn't going to be a bit of bland PR work if she could help it.

Ben kept a discreet distance between them as he walked her out to the car park through the teeming rain, but the umbrella he held over them both created an uncomfortable sense of intimacy, and the space they both, Sophie was sure, were careful to create as they walked bothered her more than the momentary touch of his hand. It seemed so much more deliberate, and therefore of far more consequence.

Her slight apprehension was unjustified. Sophie saw no more of Ben than a brief nod and greeting on passing until the end of the week.

She had stayed on late on Friday, involved in figures concerning what had begun as a vague idea but was rapidly taking shape and occupying every waking moment.

She noticed a glow of light under the door of Ben's office, and hearing no sound and knowing most people were long gone, she thought it had been left on in error.

She opened the door and was surprised to see Ben sitting in the pool of light cast by his desk lamp, looking at the contents of a cardboard box.

'I'm sorry, I thought your light had been left on,' she said, prepared to withdraw quickly.

'Don't go, Sophie,' he called. 'Come and look at these.' He unwrapped tissue paper from around an exquisite little silver box decorated with jewel-bright enamel and set with seed pearls, then placed it on the desk before her. 'Do you know what this is?'

'It's a vinaigrette, isn't it? For holding aromatics. It's beautiful.' Sophie turned it over and over, marvelling at it.

'Well, well! You *have* been doing your homework.' He was going on unwrapping the next object. 'This one's a Battersea enamel flacon. See the marvellous hexagonal shape? Each panel's got a different design. And look at that flower-shaped stopper. What craftsmanship!' He moved the box a little in her direction. 'Pull up a chair and have a look at the rest. We must do something with them. It's criminal to have them stuck away in the safe.'

Sophie sat down and watched his fingers . . . such sensitive, careful fingers on such a big man . . . a surprising contrast. One by one, almost with reverence, he unpacked the centuries-old things of beauty and stood them on the desk.

There was an eighteenth-century gold and enamel English flacon with a tiny dove poised on its stopper; an exquisite silver Regency one with tiny filigree silver doors that opened to reveal a miniature of a man's head; a quaint Dresden one with two mouths and stoppers in the form of monkeys' heads... half a dozen more, all dazzlingly lovely, the final one being a porcelain Louis XV flacon delicately painted with human figures and overlaid with a fine gold grapevine.

'All that wonderful workmanship just to make what's in effect only a container!' Sophie exclaimed.

'But a container of perfection,' Ben corrected. 'No mass production in those days, remember. Each perfume was a perfect individual blend, held by a perfect visual delight. Fitting, I think.'

'Have you been collecting them long?'

'Oh, they're not mine.' He glanced at her in surprise that she hadn't realised. 'They belong to Country Connection. In other words, they're ours.'

The idea was startling. Owning the factory jointly was one thing—it was impersonal, something for the benefit of others more than for themselves. But to own this collection of beautiful things jointly with him... it worried her.

She stood suddenly and the edge of her jacket caught the vinaigrette and sent it sliding across the desk, where Ben caught it just in time before it crashed into the more vulnerable porcelain.

'Oh, I'm sorry!' exclaimed Sophie, distressed. 'How clumsy of me! I'm tired, I suppose. Too much looking at figures.'

Ben had risen too and was looking down at her.

'You're taking all this very seriously, aren't you? Too seriously, maybe. Look at these shadows...' His fingers, the long, artistic fingers she had just been watching, delicately traced the soft skin under her eyes, and it was as though time suddenly slowed down to imprint each second with compounded forcefulness as she involuntarily closed her eyelids and her sensitive flesh acknowledged his touch.

Her heart thumped with wild alarm, but her body remained as though entranced. She felt his hands on her shoulders, gripping them, then giving her the gentlest of shakes.

'You must learn to take life at a more reasonable rate,' he was saying, his voice sounding utterly normal. 'Nothing's going to go away if you don't rush at it as though there's no tomorrow. Pace yourself.'

Sophie drew in a shuddering breath and burst free of her enslaving senses.

'I suppose I must,' she said shakily. Then, with a great effort, 'These really are wonderful. Why don't we make a display space for them? A cabinet or something—maybe in the boardroom?'

'I was thinking along those lines when you came in. We'll talk about it. In the meantime, off you go. See that you relax tonight. I'll put these safely away.'

In her mind as she drove to Carreg Plas, Sophie replayed the scene, coming to a halt each time at the touch of his fingers and her inexplicable reaction.

Ridiculous! She had behaved like some blushing maiden from the time of the vinaigrette. And she wasn't like that. But it had all happened so quickly in spite of that strange slowing-down sensation. She couldn't possibly have stopped him.

Rubbish! the reviving no-nonsense Sophie inside her mocked. Face up to the unpleasant truth, girl. For that brief moment you were Margo all over again. A man touched you . . . and you didn't want to stop him.

CHAPTER FOUR

'WHAT EXACTLY are you doing with yourself all the time?' Ben asked Sophie, rather curtly it seemed to her, on one of the rare occasions when they met outside the main door early in August.

'Still working hard at getting to know the ins and outs of this business. I'm not wasting my time,' she told him, thinking that the gold-rimmed spectacles he had forgotten to take off when he left the lab gave him an unpleasantly authoritarian air.

'I didn't say you were.' As though he read her thoughts he removed the offending glasses and tucked them in his pocket. 'I wondered if you were any nearer to finding a niche for yourself. You must come to the end of all that dusty old research some time soon, surely? What about the idea I put to you? You've been very quiet on that score.'

'I shall be ready to talk to you about it soon. In fact, I'll give you a deadline now. By the twelfth—that's when the board meeting's scheduled, isn't it?—I'll have come to a decision. You know I've been going out on calls with Owen quite a lot? We're due at Lindiswood House this afternoon, as a matter of fact.'

'He mentioned it. He also told me you get on very well with the customers you meet, which seems to be relevant. Incidentally, the board meeting's not exactly gripping stuff—just routine reporting.

There's no need for you to attend if you prefer not to. You'll get full minutes.'

Sophie wondered if he had any reason for not wanting her there. She certainly had the strongest of reasons for attending. She had decided that *that* was when she would put forward her ideas for the company and reveal for the first time that she was not quite so green as she was thought to be.

'Oh, I think I should be there,' she said with a little smile.

'Fair enough. Don't say I didn't warn you.' He headed for the production plant, raising a hand in farewell.

What did *he* do with himself? Sophie wondered. Not here, because here it was obvious that he was totally bound up in his work. But after working hours...and at weekends. As far as she could gather there was no particular lady friend—none worthy of gossip, anyway. True to his word, he had made no further suggestions of joint lunches, and all she had gleaned about his private life from Owen Davies was that he was a keen walker and sportsman, and a sailing enthusiast. The house he now lived in was near Llangorse Lake where he kept a boat... quite an isolated place, Owen said.

Irrationally, although she had been wary of too much attention, the little notice Ben paid her had rather piqued Sophie. She was his partner, and yet he seemed quite content to let her jog along doing her own thing as long as she didn't get in his way. This morning's questioning had been very much the exception.

In her office she unlocked her desk drawer and took out a file containing the work that had been occupying her, a smile playing round the corners of her mouth. She was really looking forward to the twelfth of August. From her conversations with Owen Davies, she knew that he had vague feelings that the company needed a new direction, and she hoped she would be able to count on his support against Ben's guaranteed disapproval.

The phone rang, and Sophie picked it up. It was the call she was expecting.

'Miss Pryor? Antoine Sanchot here. I have the samples you asked for.'

'Good. I shall come up to town tomorrow. Give me a time—after ten, preferably.'

'Shall we say eleven? I think you will be pleased with the changes made to the original blend...' Satisfaction and concern vied with each other in the heavily accented voice. 'I must stress, though, that I have never worked at this speed. Adequate testing requires another three weeks at least.'

'I know, and I appreciate it. We'll talk tomorrow.' Sophie didn't want to risk the conversation being overheard. She felt an exultant thrill as she put the phone down. That was the last piece of her plan falling into place. She had everything she needed now. Once she was back from London tomorrow, she would be ready. Ready to give complacent, conservative Ben Ross the surprise of his life.

She did an impulsive twirl across the office floor, then stopped. What a ridiculous rearrangement of priorities that was! What she was eager to do was make her mark on Country Connection, help the business her father had left her to take a step forward away from its rather cosy past into a more successful future. The effect on Ben Ross was quite coincidental. Of course it was.

The twelfth of August dawned grey and threatening, with the rumble of thunder in the air. Sophie went up to the boardroom early and placed her case in which all the components of her proposal were assembled beside the chair where she was to sit. The agendas were already in place, and she ran a finger down the one with her name in the top corner. Any other business... That's me, she thought.

The display cabinet for the collection of vinaigrettes and flacons was in place against the end wall, concealed lighting bringing the colours of the enamels to vivid life against the black velvet setting and sparkling off the gold and silver.

'Well, at least we agreed about that,' she told herself.

It was too hot for a suit, and she was wearing a black silk dress with a tiny white and yellow pattern, its collar and floppy bow of fresh white muslin. She had taken her hair up again—it was cooler that way, anyway—and her only jewellery was the pair of jet earrings that had been a lucky find one Sunday in Petticoat Lane street market.

There were seven names set round the table, so at least there was no possibility of a hung vote. Someone would have to have the deciding voice—in this case Colonel Williams, who was apparently taking the chair. Sophie knew that he was the original owner of the land on which the factory stood, but he was an unknown quantity since she had not yet met him. His title was not encouraging,

with its suggestion of an old diehard, but hadn't
Ben Ross himself remarked on her ability to make
a good case for herself? Today he was going to see
that quality in action. Sophie straightened her slim
shoulders and tucked a strand of silky hair back
into place. Footsteps were approaching, and she
walked lightly over to take her seat.

Ben and the Colonel were first in, and Sophie
was introduced. He was not quite as she had
expected...shrewd rather than bluff, his manner
quiet and thoughtful. Owen followed within
seconds and began placing additional sheets of
figures round the table, then Emlyn Jones, the
Production Manager, with the two factory floor
members of the Board, both of whom Sophie knew
from her time spent observing the different pro-
cesses. The woman, Margaret Clifford, was in her
twenties, she judged, and might therefore be open
to new ideas and glad of change. The man, Rhys
Howard, was one of the longest-serving workers at
Country Connection, and a very different proposition, Sophie felt. But there was really no telling
what reaction to her proposal would be. She settled
back in her chair and prepared to sit quietly through
the initial stages of the meeting. It was going to be
very interesting. Very interesting indeed.

At last the moment Sophie was waiting for was
near. The routine business and reports had been
dealt with: the workers' complaints and suggestions had been put forward and exhaustively
discussed.

Colonel Williams looked at his watch.

'We seem to have made good progress. We are now up to Item Nine on the agenda—Any Other Business.' He looked round the circle of faces. Ben Ross was already gathering his papers prior to putting them away, and heads were shaking perfunctorily.

'Yes. I have something to say,' said Sophie, and suddenly everyone was looking in her direction.

She sat forward on the edge of her chair as the Colonel said quietly, 'Go ahead, Miss Pryor.'

'So far,' she began, 'I've been very much in the position of an observer at Country Connection, watching what goes on, learning as much as an observer can learn of the production methods, reading up on the company's history. Now I have to find for myself what it was always intended that I should have—a valid, useful place in the working of the company. I say "intended", because at my uncle's insistence,' her voice hesitated perceptibly over the word 'uncle', '—for the past two years I have been following a course in Business Studies with emphasis on Marketing at the South Bank Polytechnic in London. The purpose of the course was not clear to me at the time, although I appreciated that it could be useful in many ways. But Charles Curtis's will explained everything. He wanted me here…and in an active capacity.'

Sophie forced herself not to dwell on Ben Ross's face as she looked round the table. She knew he was staring at her, a frown knitting his strong eyebrows, his eyes cold and impenetrable, and if she allowed herself to give him more than a passing glance she would falter. Owen Davies was looking humorously expectant, the others slightly bemused but interested.

'I must say that I'm impressed with Country Connection,' she went on. 'It's a happy business with excellent products and no wasted manpower in any area. I've visited many of the outlets with Owen Davies, and it seems to me that no amount of quantitative and qualitative analysis will lead to any great expansion in marketing our existing products. We are not a mass-market company: I've been told this, and I've seen it for myself. We have a steady, specialised market that will probably go on existing without elaborate promotional efforts.' She did, then, glance at Ben. His expression had not changed. After the briefest pause, she went on, 'All of which leads me to think that expansion— and I think you will accept that some expansion must take place or regression will only too easily set in—must be in a new area.'

There was a sudden sliding of papers from Ben's hands, and Sophie paused as the people on either side of him reached down to help him pick them up.

'Do continue, Miss Pryor,' Colonel Williams invited when the revealing little diversion was over.

'So now I come to the area where I see a possibility of growth,' Sophie resumed. 'I've said that there's no wasted manpower here. But what I have seen is an under-utilisation of manufacturing time. Lines stand idle because the close analysis of supply and demand shows that manufacture of a particular product is not required.'

'Over-manufacturing, to anyone who knows the business, is counter-productive. We went into all that, I thought.' The scathing interruption from Ben cut into Sophie's words, but she addressed her answer to the Chairman.

'If the board would hear me out, I'll be glad, of course, to answer any questions and have my proposals put to general discussion.'

'I think we'll agree to hold questions until an appropriate point,' the Colonel replied with a firm look at Ben, who gave an ungracious shrug and sat back, arms folded. There was a rumble of thunder, nearer now, as though the elements were reflecting the conflict building up in the boardroom.

'Competition with the big perfume manufacturers is out of the question—we have neither their promotional budget nor their production capacity. But there is one special area of the perfume market that my research suggests has not been catered for at all: namely, the first perfume buyer...the teenager. And that is the target towards which I believe Country Connection could successfully aim.'

Sophie reached for her case and opened it on the table. 'I have a mock-up here of a proposed bottle and packaging for this market, with the suggested name Chica—this links reference to girl and to glamour.' She took out a handful of blotting paper testers and began to apply perfume from her sample bottle to each before passing them around. 'This is a floral aldehyde...new, light and appropriate...and blended by Antoine Sanchot.'

'You actually approached someone like Sanchot! Who, may I ask, is financing this little venture?' Ben asked icily, unable to control himself any longer. 'Not Country Connection, I hope.' He shot an exasperated look at Colonel Williams. 'I'm sorry, Mr Chairman, but this really is beyond the pale. Miss Pryor takes too much on herself.'

'No, not Country Connection,' Sophie said calmly. 'All my specially negotiated expenses so far have been met from my own pocket, of course. If we go into production, Monsieur Sanchot is willing either to discuss a more appropriate fee, or to agree to a share of profits. He thought the experiment worth the risk,' she added pointedly.

'I must say,' said Owen Davies, examining the various samples, 'you've wasted no time in the four or five weeks you've been here, Sophie. I take my hat off to you.'

'She'll probably have the shirt off your back as well, given her head, before she's finished,' Ben said tersely. 'Have you any idea what it takes to get a new product off the ground? Do you know that the big boys spend a million pounds a year promoting their existing products—another million on top of that to launch a new name into a reputable established market like Dior? You've spent enough time studying the figures. How on earth do you imagine we can join in that kind of competition?'

'I don't,' Sophie said flatly. 'I agree that marketing eats up the biggest part of the budget. But what I want to propose cuts out the need for marketing.'

'Speaking from a lifetime in sales, I don't see how you can do that,' said Owen Davies.

'You can if you enter the market on the back of an existing product: in this case, First fashions.'

'Could you explain?' the Colonel asked. 'I'm afraid the name is new to me.'

'It's girls' clothes, isn't it?' Margaret Clifford spoke for the first time. 'They've got a department to themselves in Eldridge's in Cardiff. My sister's girl's mad on them. I like this perfume, by the way,' she added, sniffing the tester. There were one or two nods and murmurs of agreement round the table.

Sophie smiled. 'Good. Yes...First are taking off in a big way. They're establishing individual shops now, all over the country. It's a planned programme of expansion, and I think we can feature in it.'

'I fail to see what they have to do with Country Connection,' Ben persisted, refraining from any comment on the perfume though he had been holding the strip to his nose.

'I happen to know Caroline Kent, the daughter of the people who started First. I did quite a bit of modelling for her family at one time when we were at school together. I've talked to them in the past few weeks. They want to establish their own line in cosmetics and toiletries for their shops. They're willing to have us supply the perfume and one or two related products. They approve this sample— and someone else will produce it for them if we don't. They suggest give-away samples with every First garment as a promotion, and the perfume would be marketed under the First brand name.' She looked Ben full in the eyes for the first time. 'So if the venture failed, it wouldn't reflect on Country Connection—and without the hassle of marketing you know it wouldn't cost us a prohibitive amount. The raw costs of a ten-pound bottle

of perfume—and we wouldn't be remotely near that
selling price—can be as low as twenty pence.'

'And what about packaging?' His dark eyes held
hers unrelentingly. 'You probably don't realise that
new lines call for expensive new plant. This isn't
some kids' game, you know.'

It was clear that he thought he had got her, but
Sophie picked up the bottle and carton, the latter
beige with a black and white zig-zag slashing across
it and the name 'Chica' in red shadowed in gold,
dramatically different from the muted pastels of the
floral decorations that formed the background for
the Country Connection lines. 'These are exactly
the same as our existing shapes. The colouring and
the large new top on the bottle create the impression
of difference.' She gave him the sweetest of smiles
and tried not to flinch at the furious return look
he flashed at her, then addressed the whole board.

'I appreciate that this is a big question, Mr
Chairman—too big, I'm sure, to be decided today
without pause for serious thought. I have projected
production figures here which can be studied at
length,' Sophie bent over her case, getting out
papers, 'and the formula for Chica which Mr Ross
will want to see.' She passed the sealed envelope
across to Ben, who left it on the table in front of
him, then Sophie sat back and made her closing
remarks. 'If the idea I've put forward meets with
your approval, I would like to make it my concern.
It would be an area of Country Connection's work
that would be challenging for me, and it would
provide me with work that would not interfere with
what's already going on in a very well-run factory—
an important consideration for me as a newcomer.'

There was a little silence, then the Colonel spoke.

'Well, Miss Pryor, you see you've stunned us all with your proposal. Are there any immediate questions?'

The Production Manager spoke up first. 'It's obvious that if we went ahead we'd need more staff. We couldn't run all lines continuously with our existing work force.'

'That would be good, wouldn't it? For Llangellert?' Sophie said quickly. Ben could hardly deny that, however much he might glower.

'If we start getting too big we'll be a different company entirely,' Rhys Howard put in doubtfully. 'It's all very well talking about expansion, but the place Mr Curtis envisaged when he started Country Connection was the place as it is now, if you'll forgive me, Miss Pryor.'

'I go along with that to some extent,' Owen Davies said, surprisingly. Sophie had been so sure of his support. 'Up to now we've always had sole control of our own products, but this would mean an opening up to other people's standards, wouldn't it? I don't know about that.'

'But don't a lot of companies do it?' Margaret Clifford countered. 'You hear of internationally-known names manufacturing under licence for other people—and surely good standards can go out from us, not just lower standards come in.' She flushed, as though surprised by her own words. There was no question that she was a supporter of the scheme, Sophie thought. The only certain one so far.

'Mr Ross?' the Colonel queried.

'No further comment at this stage. I suggest we all need a bit of cool thinking time,' said Ben, gathering his papers together for the second time. 'Could I suggest that we fix a further meeting for Monday and take a vote then after giving ourselves the chance to absorb this somewhat startling scheme that our young newcomer to the board has put before us?'

A slight raising of the Colonel's eyebrows acknowledged the acid reference to Sophie. 'I should think that's the only thing to do. Shall we say the same time on Monday? Anyone with prior commitments?' He looked round, then noted the date on his papers. 'I now declare this meeting closed. We reassemble on Monday the fifteenth at two p.m., and I know I don't need to stress that today's proposal must remain a matter of the utmost confidence.'

As the group broke up and began to drift away the storm broke and rain lashed at the windows. Left alone in the boardroom, Sophie gathered her samples together, feeling suddenly tired and deflated after the tension of the meeting. Would they accept her plan? She really had no idea. Only one thing was clear: if it depended on Ben Ross, it would be turned down out of sheer, unadulterated rage that someone should dare suggest a change in his beloved factory.

She frowned. Well, it wasn't *his* factory any longer, was it? It was every bit as much hers, no matter how much he might try to put her down by referring to her as a 'young newcomer'. That had stung, thrown into the discussion on the tail end of his remarks as it had been.

So loud was the drumming of the rain that the subject of her thoughts re-entered the room without her hearing.

'I'm damned if I'll go through the weekend without some kind of explanation from you!' Ben snapped suddenly, making Sophie jump out of her skin. She turned to face him, and if she had never seen naked anger before, she was seeing it now. 'What exactly did you hope to gain from keeping all that under wraps?' he went on. 'Were you trying to make me look a fool in front of the board? If so, you succeeded!'

Sophie stood firm, refusing to allow any trace of the nervousness that was playing havoc with her heartbeat to show itself on her face or bearing.

'The way you reacted should answer that question for you,' she said. 'I wanted to get my proposal before the board. If you'd been given the chance to shoot it down first, it wouldn't have stood an earthly chance.' Her chin lifted obstinately. 'And I happen to think that it's a good one.'

'Do you really think that if it had been a sensible proposition to increase production, those of us who have worked in Country Connection for years wouldn't have done so?'

'Maybe *you who have worked in Country Connection for years*,' Sophie echoed cuttingly, 'have lost the ability to see it clearly.'

'Whereas you, on the strength of five minutes' acquaintance with the place, think you can totally reorganise it thanks to two years' theory in some kids' college or other!' Ben snorted his contempt.

'Not "totally reorganise",' Sophie said sharply. 'My proposal is to add a perfectly feasible side-production that could not only boost profits but provide extra jobs—and wasn't that Charles Curtis's aim on founding the company in the first place? I might also point out that a newcomer I may be, but a newcomer with connections that are definitely valuable. If Country Connection doesn't take advantage of First's offer, some other company will be only too eager to do so.'

'And good luck to them!' Ben strode over to the window and stood staring out at the rain. 'What was the idea of keeping quiet about your precious Business Studies course, anyway?' he demanded eventually, rounding on her with renewed annoyance.

'You can blame yourself for that. You jumped to immediate conclusions about me and made no secret of them.' Sophie ticked off the points on her fingers as she listed them. 'I was an uncaring, money-grubbing will-chaser who was only in it for the profits to begin with. Then I was a stupid little clothes-horse who was acting on impulse and would be off back to the bright lights the minute the novelty wore off. After that I was an empty-head who had to be found some harmless, womanly little PR slot in a company that didn't have the slightest need of it. Deny any of that if you can.'

'So why didn't you tell me you had more to you than all that?'

She raised her shoulders and hands expressively and let them fall.

'Look how you react when you do know.'

They stared at each other for a moment, dark eyes locked with hazel, neither giving way.

'Look . . .' Sophie said, reaching for her file and holding it out to him, 'this contains every calculation, every bit of research, every bit of correspondence I've done. Take it away and go through it. For all I know, in your present mood you could fling the lot on the fire. I'm trusting you to give it a fair reading.'

There was a tense moment while he looked at the file, then his hand went out abruptly and he took it from her. At the door he stopped and looked back at Sophie.

'You shouldn't have sprung it on me like that,' he said quietly to begin with, then his voice rose as he concluded paradoxically, 'I'm a reasonable man, damn it to hell!'

The door slammed behind him, and Sophie sat down suddenly.

'Obviously, Mr Ross!' she said drily to the empty room.

Solid rain continued through Saturday, and Sophie, a prisoner in Carreg Plas with the hills lowering through every window, shrouded in grey mist, sank further and further into depression. She must have been mad to think she could pull off such a scheme in the conservative atmosphere of Country Connection. And what place would she have in the company once she got a firm 'no' on Monday? She had set herself up to be thoroughly humiliated.

She stared out at the dripping landscape, pitying the sheep on the sodden slopes and at the same time envying them their total lack of ability to see into the future.

The doorbell rang at seven in the evening when she was wondering how much more of the day she could endure before giving in and going to bed. With no hope of anything pleasant happening, she went to answer it.

Ben stood on the doorstep, his trenchcoat dark with rain and his hair dripping from the few yards between road and door.

Sophie stood back without speaking, and he strode through into the kitchen, tossing the file on to the table before turning to face her.

'It could work,' he said shortly. 'But don't imagine you'll have a free hand with it. I shall be leaning over your shoulder every inch of the way. Now get your waterproof and let's go have a drink and talk it over like rational human beings. This day's been a foretaste of hell!'

Sophie, by a mammoth effort of control, stopped herself from flinging her arms round him, and then racing off round the suddenly transformed house on a lap of honour.

She looked at him steadily. 'All right,' she said with superb coolness, and went upstairs to get her coat.

'And don't be so damned cocky about it!' he shouted after her.

CHAPTER FIVE

SOPHIE'S first guess had been right: it was the casting vote that won the day. With Owen, Rhys Howard and Emlyn Jones voting, albeit reluctantly, against her proposal, it fell to Colonel Williams to line up with Ben, Margaret and herself.

'You reminded me so much of Charles Curtis's persuasive powers when you were stating your case,' he told Sophie. 'If you've got his blood in your veins, it seems to me you'll make a go of it. And, as you were at pains to explain, the risks are small—always a strong point in favour of any scheme for a military man.'

Sophie felt unexpectedly emotional after the meeting, and she sat quietly looking at her father's portrait in the privacy of her office for a little while, thinking that the Colonel little knew how much of his old friend was in her.

The mood passed, to be replaced by determination to succeed, and she threw herself into her new work with enthusiasm.

One of the points thrashed out with Ben on the previous eventful Saturday evening had been an arrangement for Sophie to report to him at the end of each week and give him a full account of how things were going.

'And if you don't like the idea, you can forget about Chica altogether, because nothing—absolutely nothing—will be set in motion, agreed, or tried out without full consultation,' he had added with convincing emphasis, so she had meekly accepted his condition, half believing he would soon get over his initial prickliness and leave her job to her.

The long-standing modelling assignment, which happened to be a photographic session for a magazine feature in the family section of one of the glossy monthlies on First's new underwear range, was scheduled for the first Friday after the committee's vote, and since she was going to be in London anyway, Sophie arranged to have a working lunch with Caroline Kent, her old school friend, who was now more involved with the running of First than her parents were.

Realising that this would mean rearranging her first reporting session with Ben, Sophie went along to see him as soon as her plans were made, wanting to play fair.

'Caroline wants to fill me in on thoughts she's had about a launch party, and to finalise the various packaging designs before we begin production,' she said. 'It seems to make sense to see her that day rather than have two journeys up to town.'

Ben flicked over the pages of his appointments book.

'Fine. So what time do we leave?'

Sophie looked blankly at him. 'I beg your pardon?'

'Leave. Set off for London. On Friday.'

'You're not thinking of coming too?' Her voice rose in outrage.

'Bronwen,' he said calmly to his secretary, 'you can go for your coffee break now.' Then when the girl had left the room, he went on coolly and very, very firmly, 'Why not?'

'Oh, come on, Ben! You surely don't intend acting like a nursemaid at every business meeting I fix? Can't you see how inhibiting that would be?'

'This isn't *every* business meeting. It's the first meeting with a new associate since we made our decision. Do I have to remind you that I'm an equal partner in everything we do?'

'You're not equal at all.' Sophie stabbed a finger upwards. 'You're way up there, playing top dog, and you're never going to stop reminding me about it. Do I crane over your shoulder in the lab all the time?'

'It wouldn't do you any good if you did. That's specialised knowledge and working experience that I happen to have—and which no one else has. You, Sophie, much though it may bug that pretty little scheming head of yours, have only theory behind you. How many more times do I have to remind you of that? You need, and you *will get*, as much supervision—though I prefer to call it "back-up"—as I consider you need.'

'You're insupportable!'

'And quite inflexible.' He folded his arms and stared calmly down into her flushed face.

'I would tell you everything we discussed—every single word,' she urged persuasively.

'You won't need to. I shall be there,' he said, completely adamant. 'You really cannot expect to walk into a business with absolutely no experience and negotiate matters that could lead us into serious trouble. Either you acknowledge that and behave accordingly, or we might as well forget all about Chica as of now.'

It was clear she was going to get nowhere.

'Oh . . . very well,' she said ungraciously.

'So what time do we leave?'

Sophie stared obstinately at him. 'I don't know what time *you* leave. My other appointment is early—too early, and it's private. Lunch is fixed for one at Silvano's in Knightsbridge. The table's booked in the name of Kent. We'll meet there.'

She was turning away, but Ben stopped her.

'Sophie, we shall not arrive separately at a business meeting for which we've both travelled up to town from Wales. We shall, of course, travel up to London together. I'm quite capable of getting up as early as is required in the morning, and I'm also quite up to occupying myself while you're busy. Give me a time and I'll be back to collect you when your private business is over.'

'You're afraid I shall get to Silvano's early and say something you're not monitoring?'

'Don't be childish. There's a correct way of doing things, and turning up to a business meeting like that pair of disgruntled lovers in the chocolate ads is not it. Besides, you'll find it quite a heavy day. I want to make it that little bit easier for you by doing the driving.'

'Oh, I *see*!' Sophie couldn't help saying sarcastically. 'It's all for me, is it? I must make sure I remember that when you're breathing down my neck all the time and correcting every word I utter.'

Ben sat down at his desk and pulled the telephone towards himself dismissively. 'You'll feel much better about it all when you've calmed down and seen sense,' he said with irritating superiority as he began to dial the number.

If he was one minute later than the time they had arranged to set off from Llangellert, she would be on her way, Sophie thought determinedly as she locked the house in the early morning on Friday. The Mini was ready, filled up in the expectation of such a delightful possibility, and she wouldn't hesitate to go off without him.

She was wearing the blue tracksuit she always used for dashing around to modelling assignments, and she had a smart suit in a dress bag to change into for lunch. Her hair was burnished gold from last night's shampooing, and her basic make-up was already done. The hair, she knew from First's style in fashion photographs, would have to have the most extraordinary things done to it, but that was up to them.

One minute before time, the Rover drew up and a disgustingly cheerful Ben leapt out to open the passenger door and help her in.

'I thought I might have to throw stones at the window to get you up,' he said as they drove off.

Sophie gave him a withering look.

'If you're going to sulk, perhaps we should have some music?' he suggested pleasantly.

'I'm not sulking. I merely have nothing to say at this hour of the day—and in particular nothing facetious. Heartiness in the early hours is quite off-putting, don't you think?' She saw from the corner of her eye that Ben was grinning, unflappable in his good humour.

'So music was a good idea,' he said. 'What do you prefer? Classical, or mildly pop? I've a sneaky partiality for Elkie Brooks.'

'You actually like that kind of music?' she queried, surprised out of her hostility.

'Why not? I suppose I seem antediluvian to one of your tender years, but I'm not quite into the Darby and Joan Clubs yet.' He slid a cassette into place, and the relaxing sound of 'Fool If You Think It's Over' filled the car.

They drove along in silence until the end of the tape, when Sophie asked for the other side, and the mood that had somehow become amicable continued. At the end of the second side, Ben said, 'How about pooling our thoughts on Chica before we get there?' and Sophie found that she was sufficiently wound down to talk without irritation and to listen to his shrewd suggestions about their approach to the discussion with Caroline.

'Anything else?' he asked, when a little silence seemed to indicate that they had covered everything.

Sophie eased round within the confines of the seat belt so that she could look at him. 'Yes,' she said, 'but not about today's business. Something's been not exactly bugging me, but shall we say intriguing me all the time I've known you.'

'And what's that?' He spoke lightly, his eyes on the road ahead.

'Why *you*...?' she asked musingly. 'There's only a small management team at Country Connection. Why did Charles pick you to inherit the place? Why not leave it to everyone involved as a sort of collective?'

Nothing changed about him. His hands didn't tense on the wheel, nor did his face betray anything—but there was something. Some sharpening of the atmosphere in the car made itself felt.

Ben took his time about replying, and when he did, his answer was in the form of another question.

'Do you expect me to know that, any more than you know why an uncle who's never seen you should suddenly bring you in and make you not only joint owner but a governing factor in what goes on at the factory?'

'But at least you were on the spot—it ought to be more understandable in your case.' Sophie found herself beginning to answer her own question. 'He'd already made you Managing Director, I suppose—or maybe he just thought you were the one with the real courage to do what was best. After all, Owen and Emlyn showed what I'd call an excess of caution about Chica, didn't they? You were against it to begin with, but you had the guts to behave rationally and change your mind when you'd really thought it through.'

Ben inclined his head. 'That's generous of you.'

'Not generous—factual.'

'Well, at least you're not accusing me of fixing the will by some nefarious means. I thought that was what you were implying.'

'Oh lord, no! I wouldn't suspect even you of that!'

'I'd like that answer better without the "even",' he said drily.

Sophie gave him a quizzical look. 'You know what I mean. We don't exactly get on like a house on fire, do we?' She suddenly became aware that they were skirting Windsor. 'Goodness, are we here already? What an incredibly quick journey it's seemed!'

Ben grinned at her. 'Now that really *is* generous, coming from one who made no secret of the fact that my presence today was highly undesirable.'

'Don't push your luck,' Sophie warned. 'It won't take much to remind me of all that.'

'All right, I'll play safe. Where do you want me to drop you?'

Sophie was reluctant to name the studio and have him ask questions about what she was doing. 'In Chelsea High Street,' she said.

'Be a bit more explicit than that. I may drop you at the wrong end.'

'No, you won't. I'll tell you when we get there—don't worry,' she said.

Just before nine and in excellent time for her appointment, Ben drew up at the point she indicated, but instead of halting briefly to let her get out and driving off, he switched off the engine and came round on to the pavement.

'There's no need for all this fuss,' she said ungraciously as he handed out her dress bag and make-up case. 'You'll get yourself a parking ticket.'

'Nonsense. You haven't said what time I'm to be back?'

'Let's say twelve-fifteen,' she told him, adding an hour to the time she had been told the session would take to be on the safe side.

'A long appointment...' He glanced at the entrance beside them, and his attention sharpened. 'Elite Studios... Is this where you're going? You didn't tell me you were working.'

'Why on earth should I imagine you'd be in the least interested?' said Sophie, pressing the bell and wanting to be away from him now. 'Thanks for the lift. I'll see you later.'

The door opened.

'Hi! You're on time—his lordship's not!' the receptionist told Sophie, adding a casual 'Hello, there!' to Ben, followed by a much more aware look as his tall, broad elegance registered.

'Good morning.' Ben smiled devastatingly and seemed in no hurry to be off. 'I shall be coming back later to collect Miss Pryor,' he said. 'Maybe you could suggest a better parking place than these double yellow lines?'

'There's a pub a hundred yards down to the left from the next corner. Try there,' she said. 'You can always have a quick drink if they give you a funny look.'

Then at last he was turning back to the car, and Sophie heaved a sigh of relief as the door closed between them.

Being back in the studio with its startling contrasts between scruffy changing-room and brilliantly-lit working area made Sophie realise just how much her life had changed over the past weeks. Was she glad or sorry? A bit of both, she supposed. She was glad of the wider challenge she had found now, but all the same it was good to be back waiting for Tony, who was always late, and gearing herself up for the very active time that sessions with him always turned out to be.

He didn't turn up until almost ten—two mugs of coffee and a long quiz from his assistant about Ben

later, and when he arrived Caroline was with him,
bringing over the clothes Sophie was to model
herself so that she could sneak a bit of extra time
with her old friend.

Sophie couldn't help smiling at the thought of
Ben's reaction to that, if he knew. Not that there
was any privacy or opportunity to talk. Once Tony
got going it was all noise and action. He always
made his models move to a selection of Top Twenty
cassettes, claiming that that way provided the best,
somewhat freakish shots that Caroline preferred for
First illustrations—and it *did* work, exhausting
though it could be.

This time, more than any other, after her sedate
weeks at Country Connection, Sophie found herself
really enjoying the beat. Strident and coarse though
it was, it made her realise just how withdrawn a
time she had been going through alone at Carreg
Plas, and for the greater part of the day equally
alone in her office. It was good to let herself go to
Tony's questionable but vigorous taste in music, to
discover her body again, and really demand the
most of it.

The lingerie was beautiful—a rainbow of colours
and sensual silks, all lace and tiny ribbons and
clever, clever shaping so that the merest wisp of
fabric could mould and enhance.

The last garment to be modelled was a body-
shaper in a subtle mulberry colour of a lace so fine
as to be almost transparent, the pattern diplo-
matically woven to strategic high-points without
which Sophie, used though she was to having a lot
of her body on display on assignments such as this
one, might have had second thoughts.

'OK, Sophie, last one. Let's have fun!' Tony called from the darkness behind the camera, and unexpectedly, after the sequence of pop tapes, the precocious sauciness of a Twenties Charleston rang out.

Sophie burst out laughing, then flung herself into the spirit of the music, body, face and hands interpreting the sound.

'Great!' Tony called as the tape ended. 'I got some beauties there!' and at last the hot, blinding lights went out and the kinder studio lights were turned on.

Sophie, breathless and laughing, suddenly felt as though someone had thrown a bucket of cold water over her. Ben must have somehow slipped into the studio under cover of the general rumpus—heaven only knew how long he had been there...and a million curses on that stupid assistant for letting him in. The girl was standing beside him now, glancing flirtily up at him as she talked nineteen to the dozen, and Ben was staring at Sophie, maybe listening to the non-stop voice, maybe not, an amused smile on his face.

All the vivacity and 'go' of the Charleston was as though it had never been. Sophie felt gauche, ridiculous in her non-garment of a body-shaper with her hair in high, twin bunches tied with ribbons to match. And because his presence had somehow managed to reduce the physical activity and the professional work she had so much enjoyed to the level of the absurd, she filled with uncontrollable anger towards her intrusive partner.

'What are you doing here now?' she accused him, causing Tony and Caroline to break off their quiet conversation near the camera at the unaccustomed rudeness of her tone. 'I said twelve-fifteen.'

'And it's now twelve-thirty,' said Ben with maddening matter-of-factness as he glanced at his watch.

Caroline raised her eyebrows enquiringly, and Sophie had to introduce them, bitterly aware of how different this was from the meeting she had envisaged at Silvano's with herself coolly elegant in her cream suit, self-possessed, and impressing Ben in spite of himself. Now look at her! She was standing there, barefoot and tiny, and only just about decent, tongue-tied with embarrassment while they exchanged civilities over her head.

'Hadn't you better go and change?' said Ben with hypocritical kindness in his voice while his eyes looked her over teasingly. 'I wouldn't like you to catch a chill because of me after all that activity.'

Sophie imagined him still watching her as she strutted huffily away to the changing-room to begin transforming herself into someone who at least looked capable of taking an intelligent part in the business lunch they were heading for.

Damn that stupid girl for letting him in! Why couldn't she have kept him in Reception? Sophie thought as she furiously brushed her hair and began rearranging it.

The vision of herself as he had seen her went on intruding between Sophie's sparkling eyes and the new, svelte image in the mirror as she touched up her make-up. She could see now that Ben had had every intention of snooping from the moment when he originally began chatting up that impressionable girl—and she had been so caught up with what they

were doing in the studio that she just hadn't realised how quickly the time was going.

Caroline appeared in the doorway.

'Your dishy partner's gone to bring the car
round,' she said. 'We thought you must be about
ready.'

'Stupid man!' muttered Sophie, and saw Caroline
grinning at her through the mirror. 'Oh, not stupid
where work's concerned,' she amended, 'don't let
me give you the wrong idea. Stupid to have come
barging in here like that.'

Caroline's stylish copper head tilted thoughtfully. 'It's not like you to get in a tizz because
somebody watched you work. I'd say that you
either hate this Ben Ross's guts . . . or you care very
much what he thinks of you for a very different
bunch of reasons.'

Sophie snorted. 'You can forget about the second
option. At the moment he's driving me up the wall
supervising everything I do like an oversized nanny.'

'Go on! Don't tell me it's painful to have a bit
of attention from someone who looks like that! I
didn't know men like him existed. He could supervise me any time.'

'Oh, shut up, Caro!' Sophie said with the contempt bred of long familiarity. 'Let's go before he
comes bursting in here. But if he makes one snide
remark about this morning, I warn you that my
temper's going to snap under the strain.'

Ben didn't. He was a charming companion
throughout lunch, and when they got down to some
serious business over the latter half of the meal
Sophie found herself sneakily glad he was there. In
spite of the long advance discussion they had had

in the car, there were questions he put and points he raised that wouldn't have occurred to her, and somehow he managed to do it without talking her down or making her feel too much of a newcomer. Mentally she conceded that she did need help initially, while at the same time resolving that nothing would induce her to admit it to him. He might be playing the part of diplomatic charmer for Caroline's benefit now, but there was a very different side to his character, as she had already seen on several occasions.

Caroline had a four o'clock appointment back at her office, so by three-thirty Sophie and Ben were on the M4 heading away from London.

Sophie asked for a brief halt at the first service station so that she could change back into her tracksuit for comfort, and when she returned to the car Ben had taken off his jacket and tie, opening the collar of his shirt and rolling up his sleeves. The strong afternoon sun fell on the rich bronze sheen of his chest and forearms, and Sophie remembered what Owen had said about Ben being a keen sportsman.

'Do you do a lot of sailing?' she asked.

'As much as I can. At sea, whenever possible, but I have to make do with the lake at weekends most of the year. Why? Do you fancy doing a bit of crewing for me?'

Sophie laughed. 'I don't know one end of a boat from another!'

'You can always learn.' He didn't press the point, and after a while he put a tape on and Sophie almost dozed beside him.

She surfaced properly again when they crossed the Severn Bridge and she realised that the Rover was leaving the motorway much sooner than she had expected.

'You're going a different way back,' she said drowsily.

'Oh, you're conscious, are you?' He smiled at her sleepy face. 'You're right. I thought we'd worked hard enough to deserve afternoon tea, and I know a place in Chepstow where they'll still be serving it. Then, if you're agreeable, I'd like to stretch my legs a bit and blow away some of the motorway fumes.'

'Sounds lovely.' Sophie yawned like a kitten and began to sit up and take notice.

Tea was splendidly reviving in a hotel giving a view of the castle and offering an array of home-made cakes of disgraceful lavishness, so that the mystery walk from St Arvans further along the road up a steep footpath was welcome as a calorie-burner as well as a provider of fresh air.

At the top of the hill, their effort brought its re-wards: a superb view of the valley below in the warm glow of the evening sun with the Wye curving like a golden ribbon, holding the picturesque ruins of Tintern Abbey in one of its loops.

They stood looking down, Ben slightly behind Sophie who stood on a small rock, and suddenly from the trees through which they had climbed came the liquid, incredible song of the nightingale.

Sophie turned to look at Ben, her face glowing, wanting to know that he too appreciated this un-expected crowning touch. He nodded, smiling without speaking, and as she looked out again over the shining valley, his arms slipped around her, pulling her back against him so that his chin rested on her head.

For a moment it seemed right. Such an experience called for two human beings to draw close to each other in sharing it. But gradually Sophie realised that the physical contact with Ben was beginning to mean more than the sight and sound that had prompted it. She was growing more conscious of his warmth, of the hard power of his arms across her slight waist, of the beat of his heart quickening as she knew her own was. When his head bent lower so that she felt his lips brush lightly against her temple, then her eyelid and her cheek, she felt such a tingling awareness of his touch, such a melting response within herself, that she lost her head. She had to stop what was happening, but she couldn't find the way to do it lightly with casual words that would bring them back to the easy friendliness that had marked the homeward journey. The only way she could deal with her own feelings was to quench them with anger, directed first in upon herself, then at him.

Without moving away she stiffened with hostility and said:

'If that's why you dragged me up here, you can forget it, Ben!' Her voice and her words were a violation of the beauty they had shared, and she saw their shattering effect on his face as he spun her angrily round to face him.

'What the hell do you mean by that?'

Sophie could only go on. She stared with cold defiance at him. 'I mean that if pushing your way in to ogle someone modelling lingerie makes your imagination hyperactive, nothing doing. I told you before—sex doesn't come into my scheme of things. You're my partner. You know this business of ours inside out and we've got to co-operate ... but for work only. I'm not in the market for any other form of casual involvement.'

What he did then shocked her to the core. He snatched her from her rocky perch, holding her so that she was powerless, her feet scrabbling vainly for the ground, his arms crushing her against him, his lips forcing her head back with brute strength in a kiss that left her outraged and breathless. Then, with a slowness that was as offensive as the speed with which he had snatched her up, he let her slide down his body until she jolted on to the ground.

'Nothing too casual about that, was there?' he said harshly.

He didn't look like the man whose gentle smile had acknowledged the song of the nightingale. His anger and his size made him brutish, threatening, and it was she who had caused the change in him.

It was from this knowledge as much as from the man himself that Sophie turned and ran like a wild thing, reckless of her own safety, down the steep path.

CHAPTER SIX

EMOTIONS were too raw for anything to be said on the rest of the way home; the journey was completed in an uncomfortable silence and ended with terse goodnights from both of them.

Sophie woke in the small hours, her heart pounding as she tore herself out of a dream repetition of what had happened high above Tintern Abbey. Then she tossed and turned, too angry with her subconscious for the rebel sensations it had flung at her to be able to get to sleep again.

Convinced that she had to find something to occupy herself outside business hours, she made enquiries at the library and came away with details of two local societies she intended joining. If folk dancing and mountain walking didn't manage to sweat the stupidity out of her then she would try something else until she was cured. She didn't intend to spend all her time brooding about Ben Ross and his libido. That problem was for him to work out—but not with her co-operation.

On Monday she had barely sat down at her desk when there was a brief, imperious rap and Ben came into the office, closing the door and leaning against it. Lab coat and square gold glasses emphasised the coolness of his expression.

'Plenty of space between us, you'll note,' he said, waving a hand to demonstrate.

Sophie didn't rise to the bait. 'If you're here to be facetious, I'd appreciate it if you did it as quickly as possible,' she said. 'I've a lot to do.'

'Me too. But I think the air needs to be cleared a little between us.'

'Does it? I thought everything was quite clear.'

'So did I on Friday. But I've thought rationally since then, and there *is* more to be said, I think.'

Sophie put down her pen and leaned back in her chair.

'Go on, then.'

'First of all, I think you probably realise now that you went completely over the top and misinterpreted something that was a simple overflowing of good feeling.' He thrust his hands deep into the pockets of his lab coat. 'I mean—anybody would have felt like doing *something* to communicate. It was on a par with stroking a dog . . . tickling a cat under the chin. Since you're a woman—to all intents and purposes——' an acid note crept into his carefully controlled voice '—you got a bit of a cuddle. That's all. The evening was out of this world, the view superb, and the company up to that point upwards of acceptable. There was absolutely no reason for you to react as you did. It was a perfectly innocent gesture.'

'One person's innocent gesture can be another person's unwelcome presumption,' Sophie said shortly, neither pleased nor mollified to be lumped in a collective of domestic pets.

'As for your suggestion that I'm the kind of man who needs the titillation of sexy underwear,' Ben went on, 'that's only worthy of one word in comment: rubbish!'

'Fine, now...' countered Sophie. 'What about your reaction then, though? Find a pious explanation for that if you can.'

A flicker of remembrance did something to his eyes that she would have preferred not to see. 'Touché,' he said. 'I can only say that you deserved it.' He gave her no chance to reply. 'And now we come to perhaps the most important thing I want to say. Your problems... Don't you think you ought to see someone about them?'

'*What* problems?' Sophie exploded, knowing full well what he was getting at and fast losing her cool.

'This unnatural aversion of yours to the most harmless approach by someone of the opposite sex. You've told me the reason for it, but it really goes far beyond natural caution, doesn't it? It's practically paranoid—and I honestly do think you should do something about it.'

Sophie got up suddenly, sending her chair madly revolving as she came out from behind the desk and confronted him like a ball of fire.

'You insufferable bighead! Is this how you react to being told your advances aren't wanted? Hasn't anyone ever turned the big man down before? Well, you'd better accept this, Mr Casanova Ross. *I'm not interested.*'

He shook his head, his eyes openly betraying the fact now that he was deliberately winding her up.

'You see? Another souped-up reaction to a bit of friendly advice. All I'm doing is pointing out that you can be helped if you want to be. You don't have to go through the rest of your life with this set of complexes you've built up inside yourself.'

'My only complex is the one I've got about you and your pseudo-psychological twaddle,' Sophie said heatedly. 'I know when someone's taking the mickey. So if you've nothing to say about work, you've nothing to say that I want to hear.'

'Think about it, anyway,' he said, starting to open the door. 'And by the way, I shall be away until Friday from this afternoon, so if there's anything more you want to say, say it now.'

'Goodbye!' she snapped childishly, further incensed by the fact that his only reply was a rumble of laughter as he closed the door.

It maddened Sophie more, somehow, than the Friday evening incident that had left both of them ruffled, because now Ben was quite in control while she was fit for nothing but fuming up and down the length of the office.

In the end she calmed down, realising that the whole conversation had been so outrageous that it had at least served the purpose of erasing any lingering awkwardness about Friday... and for all his clever talk, she didn't think Ben would bother her again with his 'harmless treatment'.

The tempo of work speeded up. Production of Chica was due to begin, and there was the printing of the packaging with one of two slight amendments to the original design to organise. Caroline had suggested and it had been agreed that a discount voucher for later purchases should be offered with each tiny sample given away with First garments, so the wording of that had to be decided and the printing to be set up. Caroline too had delegated some of the launch party arrangements to

Sophie, so there was plenty of work for her to be getting on with.

Seeing Ben on Friday afternoon was surprisingly calm and uneventful. He seemed to have decided that the score was even between them, and he stuck to straightforward business discussion, which suited Sophie admirably.

The next few weeks passed quickly, with the first batch of Chica maturing in cold storage and Sophie going up to London several times for meetings with Caroline that Ben didn't see fit to supervise. She stayed on in London one weekend to look up old friends and enjoy nights out that she couldn't help wishing Ben could observe. Complexes indeed! She was perfectly capable of enjoying herself with the opposite sex—on her own terms.

In Llangellert Sophie was becoming friendly with Owen Davies's wife Glenys, a dark, quiet girl who was several years younger than her husband. They had a two-year-old son, Thomas, who calmly accepted Sophie as baby-sitter, and it was Glenys's discovery that she was pregnant again that led to an unexpected social high-spot for Sophie.

'Aren't you pleased?' she asked Glenys, who seemed rather subdued when she broke the news.

'Yes—but I know I'm going to be a semi-invalid for the first three months if I'm going to keep the baby. It was like that last time. It means going to bed in St David's where my mother can look after Thomas—she can't come here because of my father's job—and I only get to see poor Owen at weekends. Sophie, will you do something for me?' Glenys added.

'Anything I can.'

'Partner Owen for the Sports Club dinner-dance at the Lakeside. He won't go if I don't arrange it, and that means letting down the Carters. We were going to share a table with them.'

'All right...if it makes you feel better,' Sophie agreed.

'It does. You've no idea what a functional failure I feel with all these complications.'

As it turned out, the Carters themselves had to withdraw from the event. A slight accident in their car on the way to the Lakeside left them not badly hurt but sufficiently shaken to be advised to rest rather than socialise for the next twenty-four hours.

'This isn't exactly a bundle of fun for you, Sophie,' Owen said apologetically when they were seated at a hurriedly rearranged table for two.

'In my life it's the equivalent of a summons to the Palace! I haven't dressed up like this for ages. I'm going to thoroughly enjoy it.'

'You look charming. You should have a more worthy partner,' he said, eyeing her with momentary approval before going back to staring distractedly into his wine glass.

Sophie was wearing a black Italian dress, a particular favourite, that clung lovingly to the line of her body before swirling out in a gracefully flared skirt from the hip, its scooped neckline and long, close-fitting sleeves emphasising the creamy skin of her shoulders and making her hair seem to shine more brightly golden than ever.

'I'm sorry!' Owen said again, realising how unchivalrously silent he was being. 'I keep thinking of Glenys and hoping she's all right. She felt so rotten last time.'

'Don't worry,' said Sophie, leaning over and putting a hand on his. 'We'll have dinner, dance once, maybe, just so that you can say we did, then we'll call it a day.'

'You're a nice girl, Sophie,' he told her, squeezing her fingers in response.

Just then Sophie realised that they were being watched from across the dance floor. At a table for six, Ben was sitting beside a tall, vivacious girl in red who had the kind of angular, asymmetrical hairstyle that can be so cruel but on her glossy raven-black head looked devastatingly dramatic and attractive.

'Oh, there's Ben!' she said. 'I didn't realise he'd be here.'

'Neither did I.' Owen looked across and raised a hand in greeting. 'He's with Aileen, I see. Interesting... I wondered if that was still going on, but he's very close about his private life. They used to do a lot of sailing together.'

Sophie did her best to sparkle throughout the meal, but with Owen's mind hovering over St David's and her own vague unease at being across the floor from Ben, the evening hardly went with a swing. She could have sworn she felt Ben's dark gaze on her more than once, but he always seemed to be thoroughly engrossed in his companion's conversation each time she happened to glance in his direction.

The coffee and dessert stage was reached, and dancing was now beginning in earnest, so Sophie didn't see Ben coming across the floor until he was standing at the table, the white of his superbly-fitting dinner jacket accentuating his dark good looks.

'This is quite a surprise,' he said smoothly. 'Do you mind if I steal your partner for a dance or so, Owen?'

'Not at all. Share my good fortune.' Owen gave Sophie his nice, clear-eyed smile. 'I'll go and chat with Aileen.'

The band struck up a slow, dreamy waltz, and now that the serious eating was over the lights were dimmed so that the candle lamps on the tables made little glowing pools in the darkness.

Sophie felt a tremor of strange reluctance as she went into Ben's arms, then as they began to move, their steps instantly attuned to each other, she let herself relax and enjoy the dance. The top of her head barely reached his broad shoulder, and she would have had to lean back to look into his face, but he didn't seem inclined to talk. The silence that could have been awkward was smoothed into easy naturalness by the harmony of their slow movement around the floor.

As the music ended Ben looked at her. 'That was good. One more?'

'Please. You obviously like dancing.'

'With the right partner. Come outside a moment first, though. I want to say something to you.'

His hand on her arm was firmly steering her through the nearby doors on to the hotel's vine-draped terrace, and, still bewitched by the waltz, Sophie went without protest.

They walked along to the end, away from the chatting couples clustered round the door, and when they were out of earshot Ben said quietly, 'You know, of course, that Owen is married?'

Sophie was surprised by his directness into answering simply, 'Yes, I do.'

'And that his wife is pregnant and not at all well?'

'Ben!' She faced him, protesting. 'I know all that.'

'I've known the man for years and I've never seen him with anyone but Glenys. I wanted to be sure you knew what you were getting into, no matter what madness has got into him.' He was looking at her, not accusingly, but with a worried frown.

'Ben,' she repeated, putting a hand on his arm, 'it's not like you think—not at all. Glenys more or less forced us into coming tonight, to make herself feel less guilty about being ill, I think—though why she should feel like that heaven only knows. Owen's making a valiant effort, but he's only half here, believe me, and we shall soon be leaving so that he can thankfully drop me at Carreg Plas, heave a sigh of relief, and rush home no doubt to phone St David's again before bedtime!'

If Ben had said one patronising word about being concerned because of what he considered to be her emotional instability, she would have hated him for it, but his face held nothing but pure relief.

'I'm glad,' he said simply, and his genuine pleasure at the innocence of her being there with Owen made Sophie feel good too. For a few seconds they stood beaming foolishly at each other, then Ben said, 'We're wasting time. Let's dance.'

This time the tempo of the music was fast and modern, but Ben surprised Sophie by proving himself an amusing, elegantly agile partner. Who would have dreamed that the professorial, clever chemist could be such *fun*? she thought as she twirled and turned, blonde hair flying.

At the end of the number they looked at each other with breathless laughter.

'Well . . . Owen's waiting for his turn, I suppose,' Ben said reluctantly.

'And Aileen.'

He looked almost comic with dismay, as though for a moment he had forgotten his partner.

'Lord, yes, Aileen!' he said, and delivered her hurriedly back to Owen.

Seeing him at work the following morning in his clinical white lab coat, Sophie could scarcely believe the night before's transformation. Had he danced to the end with Aileen with as much enthusiasm, she wondered, while back at Carreg Plas she had been tormented by frustrated desire to go on dancing, her feet restlessly tapping as she tried to concentrate on the late film?

'Last night was good,' he said, removing his glasses. 'Why don't we do it again some time?'

He must have looked at Aileen like that, used those very words maybe, when he said goodnight . . . if he said goodnight.

'Why not? I'll keep a dance for you next year, if I'm there,' she said coolly, and saw with satisfaction that the spark left his dark eyes before he screened them behind his glasses again and went on to talk of work.

I'm well out of that, she told herself, knowing that he had been angling to fix a much earlier and more personal date. Yes, she had done well to snub him. She was glad.

A morning had never seemed longer or more dull.

Caroline came to spend a weekend at Carreg Plas. Sophie had considered it a private visit, and it was only as an afterthought that she mentioned it to Ben, who frowned as he saw that he had appointments that could not be changed for the Friday Caroline would be arriving.

'Why didn't you let me know sooner?' he accused.

'It's only by chance I've mentioned it now. She's paying me a friendly visit, that's all. I shall show her round the factory, of course, but that's nothing you need to be involved in.'

He was looking through his personal diary. 'I could manage a meal on Saturday night.'

'Why should you? I've told you—this is a personal visit.'

'No visit from someone we do business with is entirely personal, whatever your initial relationship might have been.' His pen was poised over Saturday evening, ready to capture her in the pages of his diary.

'Well, I'm afraid it's no use anyway,' she said with scant courtesy. 'Saturday evening's booked.'

'Sunday lunch, then?'

'That, too.'

Ben gave her a cold look. 'You're a poor liar. If you're going to do it, you should practice harder. You should also think with a bit more maturity about business etiquette. You've a lot to learn, Sophie.'

So had he, if he thought a couple of dances were going to make her putty in his hands!

'Where's the dishy partner, then?' asked Caroline as they left the factory on Friday afternoon.

'He's got some appointment, I believe. We don't see much of each other, actually,' Sophie said casually.

'More fool you. That's bad judgement. I'd see plenty of him if I were here permanently.' Caroline looked searchingly at Sophie. 'Who *do* you see, then?'

Sophie ticked off her social engagements. 'I haven't had time to build up much of a circle of friends,' she said defensively.

'What rot! You could have done better than that if you gave your mind to it. It all sounds dreadfully middle-aged, Sophie. Baby-sitting...folk dancing...long, healthy walks! You'll be crocheting your own vests next! What is it with you? Did they forget the sex drive when they made you or something?'

Caroline was the one person Sophie could take remarks like that from. She smiled ruefully.

'I wish they had. If you must know, I'm scared to death of going the same way as Margo. Wouldn't you be?'

Caroline thought for a moment. 'I might, at first. But by the time I got to your age with no inconvenient children and broken marriages behind me, I'd begin to think I was a different breed of person. So why don't you?'

'Scared to try myself out, I suppose.'

'Well, you shouldn't be. Why should a cow like Margo blight your life? Sorry—but she is, isn't she? And you're not. Definitely not.'

Put like that in Caroline's no-nonsense voice, it did begin to sound as though Sophie had been creating unnecessary trouble for herself. It was good to have Caroline there with her earthy humour and her aura of continuity. They had been at school together from the age of thirteen on, and there was little they didn't know about each other.

'Will you go and see my—my uncle's grave with me? I've been rather putting off going,' Sophie said suddenly. It seemed a complete change of subject, but the connection was there. Caroline knew everything about her, but she didn't know who her father really was. Maybe she would be able to tell her, talk at last to someone about this thing that had so changed her life. It seemed wrong to hide it away like a guilty secret, and yet it was so very hard to come out with the truth.

They called in at the church on Saturday morning before setting off to spend the day in the Black Mountains. Sophie had brought roses from the garden at Carreg Plas, tight pink buds from the Queen Elizabeth bush—but there were fresh flowers already there...pink and white phlox...so someone else was remembering Charles.

When she stood up from finding room for her roses in the same vase, Sophie's face reflected the odd unease the unknown other person's flowers aroused.

'You didn't really know him, did you?' Caroline asked.

'No, sadly. But he was family, and I don't have much, as you know.' Somehow Sophie couldn't talk about it now, not even to Caroline. She felt illogi-

cally as though whoever had brought the phlox
might overhear.

Sunday morning brought an unexpected and embarrassing meeting with Ben. On Saturday Sophie
had noticed the name of the village where her
mother was born, and out of curiosity she and
Caroline drove there to have a closer look before
lunch.

Sophie tried to imagine Margo in one of the grey
terraced houses, and failed. It was like trying to
picture a peacock in a backyard hen run. The
slagheaps were grassed over now, but they still
loomed with strange threat over the slate roofs.

Suddenly Caroline was squeezing her arm.

'Am I seeing things, or is that Ben?'

The familiar silver-grey car had pulled up a little
behind them in the street, and he was getting out,
juggling brown paper bags from one of which the
leaves of a pineapple stuck out.

'Whatever is he doing here?' whispered Sophie,
thinking immediately of her bogus lunch engagement which was now about to be exposed for
the fabrication it was.

'Let's ask!' Before Sophie could caution her,
Caroline was calling out 'Hello! We didn't expect
to see you paying social calls!'

Ben paused, on the point of knocking on a green-
painted door.

'I could say the same thing. How are you,
Caroline? Sophie?' He nodded a greeting and
walked towards them, directing his next remark at
Caroline. 'Sorry you couldn't dine with me last
night. Did you enjoy your meal?'

'Very much, thanks,' Sophie said hurriedly, aware that Caroline's eyes were reflecting her puzzled attempt to work out how a takeaway, eaten while they flopped in front of the television, exhausted after a day's walking, could rate as a meal worthy of discussion. 'So what are you doing here?' she added quickly.

'Calling on my sick lab assistant. He's got 'flu.'

Sophie, looking at the bags of fruit, suddenly knew who had put the flowers on Charles' grave. It was Ben, she was certain.

Caroline wasn't going to be diverted. 'I should really like to have had a talk with you, Ben,' she said, giving Sophie an 'I'll deal with you later' look. 'Pity we couldn't make it last night.'

'Or this lunch time,' he said calmly.

'Or this lunch time,' Caroline echoed regretfully, her green eyes flashing briefly towards Sophie. 'My friend here has so much exceptional organising ability. We'll have to fix something well in advance, next time I come down.' Her eye was caught by the sailing club motif on his cream sweater. 'Hey, don't tell me you're into sailing?'

'Very much so. I'm taking the boat out this afternoon.' His dark eyes lingered challengingly on Sophie's. 'If your lunch doesn't go on too long, how about joining me at the lake?'

'I think Caroline wants to leave early, don't you?' said Sophie, feeling the colour rising in her cheeks.

Long years of backing each other up forced Caroline to agree. 'Yes, worse luck.' Then devilment made her add, 'I could always change my mind, though. I'm notorious for it.'

Ben shifted his parcels into one arm and pulled a card from his back pocket. 'If you do, give me a ring before three and I'll hang on for you.'

Sophie began to say that they wouldn't be changing their minds, but Caroline reached out and took the card.

'We might just do that. And now, what about this lunch engagement you fixed, Sophie? One, wasn't it? Hadn't we better dash?'

She gave Sophie a very hard time through the pub lunch they had—a lamentable affair of microwaved convenience food.

'And you did me out of two chances of the sort of meal that lovely man would have given us, you rat! None of this rubbish for him, I bet,' she said, prodding disgustedly at an anaemic piece of chicken. 'You owe me, Sophie Pryor.'

'All right—so what can I do to make you feel better? Anything you like...' Sophie conceded.

'Nothing, right now. I'm leaving in disgust—early, like you said.' Caroline grinned. 'Actually, I've got a date tonight. You don't catch me avoiding the opposite sex. Hah!' She pointed a triumphant finger at Sophie. 'I know what you can do. You can accept an invitation from that man—the very next one he gives you. You promised anything—and that's it.'

She was safe enough, Sophie thought as she stripped the bed and put the house to rights after Caroline had gone in the middle of the afternoon. Ben just wasn't going to ask her anywhere on her own after the way she'd made it so obvious that she wanted nothing to do with him.

Consequently her confidence was all the more rudely shattered when she went to the door a few minutes later to find him standing on the step, impatiently jiggling his car keys.

'Aren't you ready?' he queried, eyeing her thin blouse and daffodil yellow cotton trousers with surprise.

'Ready?' she echoed.

'You'll need a warmer top than that. It can be very cold on the lake.'

'On the lake?' She seemed incapable of doing anything but echo what he said, but a strong suspicion was growing as she remembered Caroline's words. 'Yes... of course. You know Caroline's gone?'

'She said she was on her way when she rang to ask me to pick you up. So what's happened to the car, then?'

Oh, you devil, Caroline! Sophie thought. She could hear the whole imagined conversation in her head. Caroline had to go, worse luck, but Sophie had changed her mind... only the car was playing up. She hadn't wanted to ask a favour, but Ben didn't mind, did he? He would pick Sophie up, wouldn't he?

And now Caroline was probably laughing her scheming head off all the way to London.

'The car? Oh, I think an evil spirit got at it,' Sophie said with feeling. 'No doubt it will start like a bird next time I try it.'

'Well, let's not waste any more time,' Ben gestured impatiently. 'The best of the afternoon's going. Let's have some action. Are you coming, or aren't you?'

There were times when it was good to have your hand forced, Sophie thought. A surprising feeling of relief was sweeping through her. She hadn't known just how much resistance she had been putting up to Ben's invitations. And what did that imply? That she had secretly been very much wanting to be with him?

And why not, after all? She could almost hear Caroline saying it, egging her on with that supreme self-confidence of hers.

She gave Ben a slow smile and shrugged philosophically as she reached for her windcheater.

'All right, I'm coming,' she said.

CHAPTER SEVEN

It was fascinating just to watch Ben's handling of *Chinook* and feel the response of the boat to each sure manoeuvre of his. Although he had warned Sophie emphatically before they left the shore of the danger of being hit on the head by the boom, several times he had to repeat the warning, not knowing that he was the cause of her inattention. He had the attraction of the trained athlete, and for a while Sophie was less conscious of the lovely surroundings than of her companion, but gradually the still, golden waters of the lake in its mountain setting offered their own distractions.

'Oh, look! What's that?' she called, half rising, as she spotted an unfamiliar buff-coloured bird among the reeds.

'Duck!' Ben shouted—and just in time she realised it was a command, not an answer. He grinned at her as the blue sail swung over her head, just missing her by a hairsbreadth. 'No, not duck—bittern. They nest around here—one of the few places they still come to. Ever heard the noise they make in the breeding season? It's a most astonishing booming sound. There's a legend about the birds of this lake, incidentally. If the prince of the area commands, they'll sing to order.'

'Have you tried it? You look very much at home here.'

118

'Me? I'm no prince. Just a jumped-up commoner.'

A noisy motorboat was gaining rapidly on them, and Sophie watched the progress of the not-very-expert water-skier in its wake.

'Commoner or not, I bet you're better at that than he is,' she said, anticipating the change of tack without being warned for once.

Ben glanced aside. 'That wouldn't be difficult. He's only just about managed to get up, I imagine. Now, why don't you come back here and make yourself useful? We've got clear water ahead. You can get the feel of the boat.'

Once she was beside him in the stern, Sophie could think of nothing but the capricious belly and flap of the sail that had seemed so obedient to him, and the obstinate tug of the rudder. From time to time Ben's hands, firm and cool, closed over her own to guide them when his verbal instructions didn't manage to get through to her. It was exhilarating, but whether the reason for that lay with the boat or the man she didn't try too hard to analyse.

After a time the wind dropped a little, and it needed Ben's skill to catch enough of it to keep *Chinook* moving. Sophie inched carefully forward to her original spot and went back to her former occupation of watching him without being too obvious about it. She was glad she had come—glad Caroline had tricked her into it. Maybe this change of attitude was only temporary euphoria, but why anticipate its passing?

She realised that Ben was smiling at her.

'Enjoying yourself?'

'Wonderfully.'

'See what you might have missed?' His expression changed suddenly, and Sophie looked round to see what was giving him cause for concern. The motorboat was approaching again from the far end of the lake. The curve of the shore had concealed their position, but the man in the boat saw them in plenty of time and veered towards the centre well ahead of them. The danger didn't come from him...it came from the unsteady boy he was towing.

He hadn't anticipated the boat's move, and was not expert enough to cope with its unexpectedness. He lost the towline and continued to skim towards *Chinook*, gradually sinking, his face registering sheer panic.

Everything seemed to happen slowly, though it could only have taken seconds. Sophie's gaze was transfixed; she was certain that they were going to run into him.

She heard Ben's shout, but only subconsciously, and almost simultaneously something gave her a thump in the back and she found herself sprawled on the bottom boards, pinned down by a heavy weight.

By the time she had realised that it was Ben on top of her, the motorboat had curved round and come to a halt alongside them, the skier was hanging on to it, and the boatman was shouting, 'Sorry about that! Everything OK?'

Sophie wriggled into a sitting up position and called, 'Yes, thanks,' not at first realising that Ben seemed strangely reluctant to move. 'At least, I think so,' she added apprehensively. 'Ben? Ben, are you all right?'

'I saw the boom give him an almighty crack as he leapt forward—to push you out of the way, I think,' the man said over the impatient snicker of the throttled-back engine. 'There was a freak gust just as he changed tack to miss us, otherwise he'd have been fine.' He craned over the gap. 'Not out, is he?'

'No, I'm not,' Ben said groggily, beginning to sit up and grope his way back to the stern. He looked as though a grey wash had been put over his tan.

'Let me tow you back,' the boatman urged, concerned.

'Not necessary. I just need a minute or two to recover.' He looked as though an hour or two would be nearer the mark. He also looked very displeased, and Sophie, aware that she was part cause of what had happened, felt totally helpless and didn't dare speak.

'If you're sure, then.' The sound of the boat's motor rose and quickened. 'Sorry again. He's just a beginner, as you might have guessed.'

The boat chugged away, the skier aboard, having obviously decided that he'd had enough for one day. Sophie was watching Ben.

'You should have let them tow us back. You really do look groggy,' she said after biting her tongue for anxious moments. 'You know we must go back, don't you, I hope? Whether you admit it or not, you took a terrible blow then. You should be lying down now. Don't make me feel any worse than I do by trying to go on, please.'

'Damn stupid business!' muttered Ben. He was peering ahead, rubbing his forehead, and after a little silence the back of his neck. Eventually he said, 'This is ridiculous. Sophie—I'm sorry, but could you come back here? I'm afraid I'm going to have to hand over to you to do your best with the boat until we're within hailing distance of someone. I seem to be seeing double—two of you, two of everything. If I don't shut my eyes and blot it out I shall make an even bigger fool of myself by being sick.'

'Oh, poor you! I'm coming.' Sophie squeezed alongside him, hoping desperately that he wasn't going to pass out in the middle of the lake where she couldn't do a thing for him. She gave him a quick, anxious look as he sat leaning forward, eyes closed, then decided that she had to concentrate on coping with the sail on the basis of her far too short period of instruction.

'Anyone near?' he asked after a few moments, attempting to look and then quickly shielding his eyes again.

'Not at the present. Don't worry, we're doing fine,' she said with considerably more confidence in her voice than she felt.

'Tell me where we are—I really haven't a clue. I'm so sorry about this.'

'*Please* don't keep apologising,' Sophie implored. 'How do you think I feel, knowing it was because you were shoving me out of the way that you got hit yourself? We've gone round in a semicircle without too much trouble, and now we're heading back the way we came. We're just opposite the inlet where we saw the bittern.'

'And my head's certainly providing the boom!' Sophie felt relieved that he was at least attempting a joke. He was silent for a while, then asked again, trying to be casual, 'Anyone near now?'

'I'm afraid not. The lake's deserted at this end. We're heading in the right direction without my doing anything much, fortunately, though.'

'All right. Then listen. You'll have to get as close as you can to the landing stage, then I'll tell you how to put the sail out of action and we'll drift in, with a bit of luck. Tell me when we're opposite the red marker buoy. It would be a good idea to keep to the lakeward side of that if you can manage it.'

Sophie glanced quickly at him, not deceived by the casual tone of the last words. What would happen if they went to the wrong side? They'd run aground or something like that, she supposed. But Ben was looking a slightly better colour, and so far so good. She concentrated on willing the boat in the right direction.

By some miracle they nudged into the deserted landing stage with hardly a bump, and Sophie heaved a sigh of relief as she tied up *Chinook*.

'How is it now?' she asked as Ben opened his eyes.

'Well, at least the two of you are closer together,' he said drily.

'Take my hand. I'll help you out.'

'I'm not that much of a geriatric!'

'Ben! Don't be stupid.'

When they were both safely on land, she asked, 'Where are your car keys?'

'Here.' He handed them over without demur this time. 'Just get me home. All I need is to lie down a bit. What a farce of an afternoon!'

'I think you ought at least to get yourself checked at the nearest accident unit,' she insisted anxiously.

'Sophie, I've got a doctor living in the next house to mine if it's necessary to see someone—which it isn't. This is only temporary. I'm not unfamiliar with what can happen in yachts, you know.' Ben put an arm on her shoulders and she got him into the passenger seat without too much difficulty.

Fortunately he had pointed out the lane leading to his house when they were nearing the lake, and managing the Rover after the unknown quantity of *Chinook* was child's play—much easier than negotiating the narrow stairs in the cottage up to Ben's bedroom.

'Take the car,' he said as she was slipping off his trainers. 'You can come and pick me up for work in the morning. At least it'll save you the hassle of wondering if your car will start. Oh... God!' He sank back on to the pillows, and Sophie swung his legs on to the bed. 'What a waste of what I thought was going to be a pretty miraculous afternoon! I should have known it was too good to be true, you saying yes for once. You must think me thoroughly stupid.'

Sophie looked down on his closed eyes. 'If you think I'd think that, then you must think *me* thoroughly stupid!' She pulled up the bedclothes, then brushed back his hair in a gesture that was at first utterly instinctive, then sent a shock of surprise through her as her fingers felt the shining crispness of his hair.

His eyes were open now, and his hand came up to close on hers.

'Thanks, Sophie,' he said drowsily, turning his head into the pillow and seeming to fall instantly asleep so that she couldn't be sure afterwards if it was by accident or design that his lips brushed against the palm of her hand before he let it go.

She went quietly downstairs, and the slim grandmother clock chimed a silvery six as she reached the hall.

She was *not* going to leave Ben alone in the house. She would give him a time to sleep, then if his vision was still affected, she would get the doctor neighbour round whether he liked it or not.

The house was like Ben, she thought. It gave little away. He had moved in in something of a hurry, of course, and the furnishing looked that way—good, but neutral and lacking in the individual touches that make a place indicative of its owner. Although, as far as she was concerned, this bland, impersonal place *was* indicative of the man she knew so little about. There wasn't a single photograph on display. The twin oatmeal settees were grouped so that the view of the lake and mountains was the focal point of the room, and for a while Sophie sat watching the sun sink lower. She found *A Pale View of Hills* on the bookshelves and tried to read, but she couldn't really concentrate.

The doctor's house... She went out into the garden. There was only one house in sight, so that must be it. There was a car in the drive, so he was in.

She went back restlessly into the kitchen, and for a while occupied herself making soup with a partly-

eaten chicken she found in the fridge. At least there
would be something nourishing and easily digest-
ible when Ben surfaced again. She prepared a tray,
and drifted into the sitting-room again, but it was
no good. She couldn't just sit around wondering if
she had done the right thing. It was seven-thirty.
Supposing the doctor went out for a meal?

She set off across the hillside and in twenty
minutes was back with the doctor—Steve Vincent,
he told her, surprisingly un-medical-looking in his
jeans and sweater, but jolly and reassuring. She had
done absolutely the right thing in calling him, he
told her, and he repeated it loudly and firmly when
Ben began to protest in a very bad-tempered way
on being roused.

'I'll leave you to it,' said Sophie, avoiding Ben's
eyes and running back downstairs to wait for the
doctor's opinion.

'Disgruntled but otherwise fine,' he said cheer-
fully, popping his head round the door some quarter
of an hour later. 'The visual disturbance has gone
now, and there are no signs of concussion. You can
sling a bit of light food at him to sweeten him up
a bit, then after a night's sleep he should be absolutely back to normal. Ignore the growling. He's
a strong fellow, and they don't take kindly to being
caught at less than peak fitness.'

'I'm very grateful,' Sophie told him. 'I just
couldn't stop worrying that we should have gone
straight to the nearest hospital.'

He was scribbling on a prescription pad. 'This is
my phone number—but I'm sure you won't need
it. He'll sleep like a baby. Hang around tonight if

you want to—but more for your own peace of mind than because it's actually necessary.'

Sophie went out with him and stood talking for a moment or two, then, rather apprehensively, went upstairs with the tray.

Incredibly, Ben was asleep again, his lashes long and dark against the smooth brown skin under his eyes. She stood staring at him. His mouth, relaxed from the firm line of wakefulness, looked strangely sensual, and along the line of his jaw the darker, rougher skin that no doubt got an evening as well as a morning shave gave him a vulnerable look. But his chest was rising and falling with reassuring, slow steadiness. It would be silly to disturb him again when she knew that he was all right, and sleep was obviously what he needed more than anything.

She went back downstairs and ate the chicken soup and bread and fruit herself, then, after getting a blanket from the spare room, she curled up on one of the settees with a lamp near her head and the Ishiguro to read. She wasn't going to sleep, of course, but it might be chilly in the night.

The print danced and blurred after a while, and Sophie rubbed her eyes, fixing them determinedly open as she went on reading.

The birds were singing and the sky was hazy, early-morning blue through the window. Sophie leapt to her feet. A fine nurse she was! It was after six— and not once had she roused and wondered how Ben was.

She went cautiously upstairs and looked in through the bedroom door. His back was towards her, and the shoulder she could see was bare . . . so he must have got up and undressed at some point, but he looked so very still now. She couldn't see any sign of movement.

'Ben?' she whispered, then a bit louder, 'Ben?' Nothing happened.

He was sleeping soundly, that was all—and it was ridiculous to have this fluttering feeling in her throat.

She went over to the bed and leaned over him, trying to see his face, but his arm was flung up on the pillow and his face buried in the crook of it. The bed was tight against the wall, so there was no going round the other side to see more clearly.

Sophie leaned further over, one hand on the mattress beyond Ben, her head close to his as she tried to detect some slight sound of his breathing to reassure herself. Her cheek brushed against his shoulder. It was warm—thank God for that!

Then she gave a muffled scream as a hand shot out from the bedclothes and grabbed the arm on which she was balanced, sweeping her forward so that she tumbled in a clumsy heap and rolled to the inside of him, ending up looking into a very much alive and wide-awake face that was grinning wickedly at her.

'You pig!' she gasped when she had enough breath to speak, though she couldn't help smiling with relief as she flopped back against the pillow. 'I was terrified you'd gone and died on me. I take it you feel better?' she added drily.

'Fit as a fiddle, so you can relax and stop worrying. Perhaps that's superfluous advice, though, judging by the way you slept soundly all night.'

'How do you know I did?'

'How do you think your lamp was turned off?'

'You came and sneaked a look at me?' Sophie said indignantly.

'Not intentionally. I didn't know you were there, remember. I came down for a drink and there you were with the light on and a book sliding out of your fingers.'

'And my mouth open, I suppose?'

'You were sleeping very sweetly. It seemed a bit unnecessary to wake you up and tell you I was fine when you obviously were very relaxed about it all.'

'I *did* stay!' Sophie protested.

'If only for a good night's rest.'

'And I made soup and brought it up as soon as the doctor had gone. *You* were fast asleep then.'

'But I heated it up when I'd had my drink, and very good it was too.'

Sophie was just beginning to think how very odd it was to be lying there side by side with Ben in— or at least on—his bed, when he turned to smile a lazy smile at her.

'Well, isn't this cosy?' he said. He shifted slightly to lean on one elbow and the bedclothes slid a little further down. Sophie speculated briefly on what exactly—if anything—he was wearing. That look on his face seemed to suggest that he was the kind of man who wouldn't have a clue what pyjamas looked like. She blinked her eyes hurriedly against the far-too-close expanse of muscle and dark hair and suntanned, surprisingly satiny skin. She could feel her face beginning to go hot, and she sat up purposefully.

'It's not cosy. It's ridiculous!'

'Don't go.' His arm pulled her down again. 'I want to talk to you.'

'I can think of more suitable places.'

'Don't be stuffy. I said "talk".' The arm that had pulled her back had somehow ended up around her, pillowing her head, and his hand was stroking her hair in a very hypnotic, persuasive way.

Sophie swallowed. 'What do you want to say, then?'

'That's better. Only this: I think that yesterday we began to break through some kind of barrier. I don't want those defences of yours to go up again.'

She tensed, ready to move away again, and his hand gripped her shoulder, giving her a little shake.

'Don't do that!' he scolded. 'What do you think I am? Some kind of unprincipled lout with too much brute strength for his own good?'

Sophie steeled herself against her own body's alarming inclination to snuggle up to him, and managed a cool sideways look.

'This is hardly your average recommended situation for a girl, is it?'

'And you're not anybody's average girl, are you? You don't allow yourself to have the normal range of feelings—you more or less told me so yourself, so it's no good going all prickly and stiff like that. All I'm trying to say is that yesterday, up to that stupid business with the motorboat, you seemed for once to be behaving normally. You were—for want of a better word—friendly.'

'And now it would suit you very well if I were decidedly friendlier,' she said coldly. 'I've got a perfectly normal range of feelings, I'd have you know. Where I differ, no doubt, from your usual kind of willing girlfriend is in how I choose to deal with them.'

'Really?' His eyes were glittering dangerously. 'So if I were to do this——' he leaned over and kissed her quickly on the lips, and then, taking advantage of her surprised stillness, kissed her again, not so quickly '—you might feel something?' he concluded, looking down at her with false innocence.

Sophie knew somewhere in the cloudiness that was filling her mind that now was the time to move while she still was capable of it, but a heavy lethargy had begun to invade her, and his taunt about normal feelings had gone home.

'Well...did you?' asked Ben softly.

'Something.' She tried to compress the world of sensations fighting through her bloodstream into one cool, blasé little comment, but her voice came out stupidly squeaky and she made the mistake of looking directly at him. He had been teasing her, but as they looked silently into each other's eyes, something changed.

Ben gave a smothered exclamation and pulled her towards him, burying his face in her neck so that she felt the roughness of his early morning skin and found that it added devastatingly to her sense of being swept along by some raging current over which she had no power.

'What is this knack you have of making me do things I have no intention of doing?' he muttered, his voice smothered and warm against her skin. Something made her want to tell him that it was all right...she felt the same bewildering compulsion that he did.

She softened against him, and slowly, as though they had independent life, her hands slid up the warm, smooth skin of his back, discovered and lingered in the unexpected silkiness of his dark hair. She remembered with a pang the blow to his head, and her fingers curved tenderly round the nape of his neck while her lips pressed against the soft skin under his ear.

'Sophie——' His arms tightened round her, and for a moment longer she felt a fierce desire to let herself go, surrender to the host of new, over-powering sensations clamouring to be given rein. So it was this that had defeated Margo...this blazing, dazzling, wonderful——

The thought of Margo was enough. Suddenly Sophie's hands were pushing roughly against Ben's chest, and as his startled hold on her slackened, she scrambled inelegantly over him and thudded down on to the floor.

'No, Ben,' she said from the doorway, flushed and breathless. 'Not as easily as that.' Then she ran across the small landing into the bathroom and locked the door.

She sat on the edge of the bath, crossed arms hugging herself, willing sense back into her head and at the same time half expecting Ben to come thundering on the door. But nothing happened.

Soon, in the stillness of the early morning, she could hear the sound of the bedroom's en-suite shower running, and she realised that he was going on with the business of getting up.

So that was what she would do, as though nothing at all had happened. She ran the bathwater and splashed around noisily in it for as long as she could, trying to work up sufficient bravado to face Ben again, and wondering what on earth people said after an unscripted scene like the one she had just escaped from.

When she walked into the kitchen, though, all her planning proved unnecessary.

'Black or white?' Ben asked calmly, lifting the coffee pot. He was dressed for work in grey slacks, white shirt and dark blue tie, his hair sleek from the shower, and the jacket of his suit was on the window seat. His expression was as immaculately correct as his appearance.

'I thought you might run me home,' Sophie said stiffly, standing in the doorway.

'I made breakfast for both of us.' He waved a hand at the table. 'Muesli, grapefruit, toast if you want it. It makes more sense for me to drop you at your place on my way to work, and look at the Mini at the same time, if you don't object.'

Sophie shrugged. 'All right.' If he could be cool, then so could she. 'Black, and muesli, please, then,' she said.

She carefully avoided his eyes while she ate her breakfast, and she had no idea what was going on in his mind until they finished eating and he said, 'Well, don't you want to know what I think?'

'No.' Steam had been building up in her while she ate. 'But I'll tell you what *I* think. I was absolutely right in the first place to say we should stick to a working relationship. I don't like your games, Ben.'

'I don't play any games that my heart's not in.' He looked at her enigmatically. 'One day that obstinate mind of yours, whether you like it or not, will stop putting the brakes on the rest of your senses, and let you start living.' There was the slightest of pauses, then he said briskly, 'Shall we go?'

At Carreg Plas Sophie threw him the briefest of thanks over her shoulder as she unlocked the door and went in to change while Ben took the keys of the Mini. She heard the engine start up after its customary hiccup as she pulled a crisp emerald green cotton dress on—there was no reason why it shouldn't start, of course, and she assumed that Ben had gone straight on to the factory in his own car.

But when she came downstairs he was in the sitting room, looking at a photograph of Charles that she had found in a drawer and put out on one of the shelves.

'The Mini seems to be all right,' he said absent-mindedly, then he turned round, the photograph still in his hand. 'You know, it wouldn't surprise me at all if Charles wrote his will with the sly hope that we'd end up as more than joint owners of Country Connection. He was a shrewd operator, if a quiet one.' Dark eyes rested on her without actually seeing her and he seemed to be talking to himself, mulling over something that perhaps the morning's happenings had put into his head. 'I can see his line of reasoning... Put us together, see what transpires, and maybe the business would end up being sure of staying in the family. An intriguing idea...'

Sophie said the most cutting thing she could think of.

'And your bread would be very nicely buttered on both sides, wouldn't it? First half the business out of the blue, then the whole lot.' She slung her bag over her shoulder. 'Personally I think I'm doing enough to please Charles without mortgaging my whole future.' Then, still smarting from his last airy words at the cottage, she echoed them sarcastically as she added, 'Shall we go?'

CHAPTER EIGHT

Sophie looked back along the neatly weeded border against the bottom wall of the garden at Carreg Plas. At least frustration of all kinds was good for something. She had pulled out every weed as though it were Ben—though he was far from being the only current fly in the ointment.

She picked up the last pile of rubbish and threw it on the compost heap in the corner, then perched on the wall looking out over the hillside, hugging her knees.

The last few weeks had been not only hard work, but complicated by snags that her own impetuous rush into new ideas for Country Connection had caused.

She had learned the hard way just why the factory had run so smoothly and happily in the days when every production line was not working full blast. With no spare capacity, unforeseen things happened, and before you knew where you were there was a log jam of work and orders compounded by the inevitable human error and mechanical breakdown. Much more forward planning was necessary, and she now understood why there hadn't been wholehearted approval of her plans from everyone.

It was going to work out all right in the end— even Ben had reassured her on that score, but in a way that, whether he intended it or not, made her feel patronised, like a child indulgently excused for immature behaviour on the grounds that she would inevitably learn one day. In the meantime, all the teething problems were making her feel decidedly humbled.

This week's problem had been caused by one of the new men recruited to meet the increased work load Chica production created. He was a different breed from the long-term employees, a highly political animal who for the first time made Sophie aware of an 'us' and 'them' mood in the factory. He had stirred up feeling about canteen facilities, and now there was strong demand for food to be available at midday, whereas before he came everyone had happily brought in packed lunches as long as plenty of tea and coffee were laid on.

Sophie, up to her ears in arrangements for the Chica launch the following week, had scant time for the idea.

'Maybe we should just get rid of him—he seems to be nothing but a trouble-maker,' she said to Ben.

'You can't get rid of a man for having an idea and wanting it to be considered,' Ben told her reasonably. 'I'm not sure that he isn't right. It wouldn't be a big thing. We've got a kitchen that's fully equipped but used only for drinks-making, a recreation room with tables in it, and with our small staff and perhaps no more than half of them wanting to take advantage of prepared food initially, one woman could probably run a limited no-choice hot meal for a trial period quite easily. We'd fix prices on a non-profit basis, just to cover her wages and basic costs. I think we should talk about it.'

He always had time to listen. Time and patience: the same time and patience that he seemed to be devoting to his pursuit of her. Regularly he would offer an invitation to a concert, the theatre, a meal—and just as regularly but not half so patiently Sophie would refuse. It was the fact of his quiet, controlled patience that annoyed her as much as anything. If you wanted a man...which she didn't...who would want this steady, calculated pursuit by someone who had more or less said outright that you were a sort of insurance policy?

'Why won't you accept the fact that it's not on?' she had asked him crossly that very evening.

'Because one of these days you're going to realise just how ridiculous you're being,' he'd answered, his eyes looking down at her with that blend of tolerance and amusement that so irritated her. He had never referred again to that silly business at the cottage after the accident, but there were times when Sophie felt sure that he was thinking about it, times when she felt his eyes resting on her in a way that made her spine tingle and her mind lose concentration.

She jumped down from the wall. And now she was wasting time in her own garden thinking about the irritation he caused her. The roses were still lovely. She remembered that the ones she and Caroline had put on Charles' grave must be well and truly withered, and decided to go up with some fresh ones. She gathered an armful of Peace, their buds tight and creamy, the opened petals flushed from lemon to pink.

The soil on the grave was hard and baked, unkind-looking. Sophie arranged her roses and resolved to bring a hand-fork next time she came. She sat back on her heels, looking at the name carved in the headstone.

'You see,' she found her inner voice saying, 'you gave me so much to cope with all at once. Love…work…a home… And now I'm being made to think that maybe you wanted to give me something else, something more complex even than all that. But that can't be part of anybody's plan, can it? Not even yours. It should happen because the two people themselves want it to; if not it could go terribly wrong and end up twisted and cruel, like it was for you. That's what I'm afraid of.'

She was almost down at the gate when, disbelievingly, she saw the grey Rover beginning to climb the hill. She had walked over, so there was no car to betray her presence, and she didn't want to see Ben—not here, where she felt so revealed and vulnerable. She ran back up the path and pressed herself against the church wall behind a buttress.

Ben stood looking down at the roses for a moment. The evening sun picked out glints of copper in his dark hair and brightened the dull gold sweater and silver cords he was wearing. He bent down and touched the roses, then straightened up and looked around.

Sophie wasn't sure if he actually said her name, but she felt it hanging questioningly on the still air and there was suddenly the most powerful, tugging force urging her to go to him. For a bewildering moment it seemed so easy and so simple and so very, very right. A heady mixture of warmth and excitement seemed to be rising up in her. Is this what it feels like to love someone? she wondered.

Then she saw that Ben was crouching down again, doing the very thing she had planned to do: he was forking over the hard soil. The coincidence was creepy, shocking her, making her feel strangely trapped. She shut her eyes and leaned back against the stone that felt almost alive from the sun's warmth, and the momentary madness drained away.

What did she know of love, with Margo for her teacher? The lessons she had learned from that particular quarter were likely to have a far more animal basis. Anyone could look at a good-looking man and fantasise . . . and nobody was denying that Ben was handsome enough.

Get out of my mind, Ben Ross, she thought savagely. What do I know of love, except that it hurts? What do I want to know?

She forced herself to keep her eyes shut until the nearer sounds stopped and then the car engine started up, and when she opened them at last, Ben had gone.

The Chica launch party was fixed for the first Wednesday in October—Wednesday in the hopes that it would feature on the Thursday fashion pages of the two daily papers whose fashion editors had been invited.

Sophie went up to London two days ahead of Ben and Owen so that she could supervise the final arrangements and see for the first time the coming together of music, dance, fashion and laser at the first rehearsal.

Caroline had taken over Pinkerton's, a fashionable West End nightclub with a floor suitable for the extravagance of presentation she and Sophie had worked out. There was to be a lavish meal for the buyers, journalists and media people invited before the show, and afterwards there would be general dancing.

The show itself featured First clothes for various occasions, atmospherically grouped, with linking interludes by a young dance team called The Preppies between each section. The high-spot was to be the presentation of a new range of more sophisticated girls' clothes that Caroline had designed specially for the Chica brand name, using the beige, black, white, red and gold Chica colours. The girls showing the range were to end by bringing in a giant mock-up of the Chica perfume box from which the young model chosen to be the Chica Girl would emerge. She was a striking, raven-haired sixteen-year-old with a long, glossy rope of hair and stunning dark eyes, and her blend of sophistication and innocence was exactly right to project the image they were seeking for the product.

Simultaneously with her appearance, a mist of Chica perfume was to be sprayed throughout the room, and the girls, still in their Chica clothes, would distribute samples and information packs to each table.

At the end of the dress rehearsal on Tuesday, Caroline turned exhausted eyes on Sophie.

'Well, what do you think? My mind's gone.'

'If it goes like that tomorrow, we'll be happy.' Sophie smothered a yawn. 'What a day! I'm bushed, Caro. I can't think of a single thing more we could do tonight. I'm fit for nothing but going back to my hotel and soaking in the bath, then

having an early night. I don't think I can be
bothered to eat, even.'

'Get something sent up and have it in bed.
Speaking of which, what time does your dear Ben
arrive tomorrow?'

Sophie sighed. 'Don't you ever stop? Ben *and*
Owen get here mid-afternoon—and how many more
times do I have to tell you there's nothing going on
in that quarter?'

'Of course not! Who am I to suspect you of or-
dinary human failings? Run along and go to bed
alone, you boring old spinster. I haven't the energy
to deal with you at present.' Caroline turned to the
huddle of tired girls waiting aimlessly for dismissal.
'Right, girls! That was fine. Five on the dot tomorrow for a last walk-through.'

Sophie picked up her things and quietly left. Back
in her room, she went through her check list once
more after her bath. Everything was taken care of,
and to the best of her knowledge nothing had been
overlooked. Spinsterish or not—and thank you for
that, Caroline, she thought, pulling a face in the
mirror—she wanted nothing more than sleep.

Nothing might have been overlooked, but the
horrifyingly unexpected was waiting to pounce
before nine next morning.

'Sophie, you'd better be feeling good
today——' It was Caroline on the phone, her voice
taut with the determined note Sophie remembered
from past tight corners. 'I've just had Tina's mother
on the line. The girl's fallen downstairs. Her
ankle's broken.'

'Oh, no!' Sophie sat back on the bed. Tina was the 'Chica Girl'.

'No chance at all of her being there tonight—in any case, what sort of image would a hobbling model convey? Anybody but her we could have covered for, but without Tina...'

Sophie was thinking rapidly. 'Can't one of the others do her routine? They're quick at picking up each other's numbers.'

'But none of them could wear Tina's clothes. The others are standard five-foot-eight size tens, remember. She's the odd one out for size.' There was a pause...a significant pause that filled Sophie with foreboding. 'She's *your* size, and *your* height, Sophie.'

'Oh, no!' Sophie surprised herself with her own extreme aversion for the idea. She seemed to have moved so far away from the world of modelling in a surprisingly short time. 'I couldn't, Caro! Not this one. And I know Ben wouldn't want me to do it.'

'I thought you didn't care what Ben thought about anything.' Caroline's voice hardened. 'This is an emergency, Sophie. You did the studio shots—why not this?'

'I was committed to do those from way back.' Sophie knew instinctively what Ben's attitude would be. Chica was a bit of a hush-hush production for the factory. If there were publicity going, he would want it to be for Country Connection products, not for something they manufactured under licence. And apart from Ben—if the press got wind of her own involvement with the factory, they would dress it up as a real-life Cinderella story...and there was so much that Sophie didn't want dragged into public view.

'I've put a lot of money into this launch, and I don't want to fall flat on my face,' Caroline was saying. It was true—and she had been more than fair all along the line. Sophie was torn two ways, and Caroline was quick to sense it.

'Have you considered that I wouldn't have anything like the right image? I don't look at all like Tina. Wrong hair, wrong eyes…it wouldn't work,' Sophie protested.

'I know that—but what else can we do? The ending would fall flat as a pancake without a Chica Girl. Sophie, you could do something about adapting the image. I know you. If you gave your mind to it you'd come up with some miracle or other.'

Sophie bit her lip for a moment, but she knew she couldn't just stand back and let Caroline down after all the hard planning.

'All right. Leave it with me for this morning,' she said. 'I've got the germ of an idea. If I can pull it off, I'll contact you after lunch and you can talk me through the routine. But if it doesn't work, we'll just have to cut the number. Fair enough?'

'Fair enough.' The phone went down rapidly and Sophie knew that Caroline was not giving her time to think again.

It seemed through an exhausting morning as though she was never going to get what she wanted, but one o'clock found Sophie dashing into the hotel again, reasonably satisfied with her efforts.

The receptionist stopped her.

'There was a message for you, Miss Pryor—a Mr Davies. He said it was urgent, and you should ring him before twelve or it would be too late; which it is, I'm afraid.'

Sophie looked at her watch. Owen with some last-minute query, she supposed. Well, she couldn't do anything about it now. He and Ben would be on their way.

On their way! She was supposed to be waiting here to meet them at four, but she couldn't possibly be. The Maison Martin man was coming here at three, then she had to see Caroline, and there was the walk-through which she absolutely couldn't miss at five.

'Could you let me have something to write a message, please?' she asked. She scribbled the briefest of notes—there was too much to attempt to explain on paper: 'Back between six and seven to change. Sorry not to be here when you arrive,' and addressed it to Ben, then made a quick and deliberately obscure phone call to Caroline arranging to see her at Pinkerton's at three-thirty. Now she had to wash her hair and sort out what she was going to do with it . . . and that meant no time for lunch, but there were nuts in the fridge with the drinks, and those would keep her going.

When Caroline walked into the changing room at twenty-five to four, her reaction was everything Sophie had hoped for.

'I don't believe it! Where on earth did Sophie find you?' she exclaimed.

The slight girl with the long, glossy dark hair, the room's only other occupant, turned and gave a shy smile. She was wearing the Chica Girl dress, which fitted her perfectly, and against its smart, dark colours her skin was flawless as cream velvet. The one difference between her and Tina was that this girl was wearing a provocative black lacy mask.

'I really don't believe it!' Caroline repeated, viewing the girl from all angles. 'And what about that mask? Why didn't I think of it? I can see the blurb we'll use right now...' She struck an attitude. '"Who is the girl behind the mask? Could it be you? Only the perfume knows the secret..."' Customer identification! She went over to the door at the back of the room. 'Sophie, you genius! Where are you?'

'Right here!' The Chica Girl whipped off her mask and tilted her wig ludicrously to reveal shining blonde hair. 'Great! If I can fool you I can certainly fool Ben and the rest. Is it on, then?'

Caroline whirled her round. 'I'll say it is. Where did you get the wig? It's more like Tina's hair than Tina's is!'

'At about the twentieth place I went to. I was beginning to despair. You've no idea of the complications, even now. Monsieur Martin's risking life and limb lending it to us, and he wants to collect it immediately after the show to correct the adjustment he had to make so that I could wear it. It's for some very important lady singing at the Royal Opera House, and if she found out he'd never get work for them again.' Sophie pulled the dark hair into position and immediately became someone else.

Caroline shook her head admiringly. 'I always said you could charm the birds out of the trees.'

'But right now it's a question of dancing. I've a routine to learn. Let's get on with it!'

When Sophie got back to the hotel, later than she had anticipated, the receptionist stopped her again.

'Miss Pryor, Mr Ross wants to speak to you as soon as you come in. He's in room 225, and he seemed a bit—you know—not too happy,' the girl confided.

Sophie smothered a groan. Her feet ached, her head ached, and in a very short time indeed she had to be glamorous and sparkling. Ben in a mood was all she needed. She pressed the button for the second floor, hoping he would have got over it.

He was still wearing the suit in which he had travelled, but he was on the point of changing because he had to go in and turn off the bathwater before speaking to her. His face was exactly as the receptionist had implied.

'No doubt London's full of old attractions for you, but I think you could at least have the courtesy to keep to the arrangements we make,' he said coldly.

Sophie was too tired to think of a clever answer. 'There was a perfectly good reason for my not being here,' she said. 'You've no idea what it's been like today, with last-minute snags and . . . things to do.'

'Did the man you left the hotel with this afternoon come into the category of last-minute snag, or was he a thing to do?' Ben queried sarcastically. 'The latter, judging by your air of exhaustion.'

The man he referred to was Monsieur Martin with whom she had walked through Reception after he had delivered the adjusted wig, and no doubt the chatty receptionist was responsible for giving Ben this information. Sophie couldn't explain about him without telling Ben she was standing in for Tina, and she didn't want to do that.

'You're being stupid, Ben,' she said. 'I've got to get ready now, and look at the time! If all you're concerned about is slapping my hand, couldn't you save it for later?' She felt a flash of anger at the unfairness of it all. 'The least you and Owen could have done was make sure there was tea or a drink or something waiting for me.'

'If you'd not been too "busy" to answer Owen's call this morning, you'd know that he's not here.'

'Not here? But we've to be at Pinkerton's at eight. What time's he getting here, for goodness' sake?'

' "Not here", as in going somewhere else.'

So that meant she and Ben were in adjoining rooms with no Owen to make it all seem safe.

'And who arranged that?' she demanded. 'When I booked these rooms it was for the three of us, not another of your cosy twosomes. Have you been trying to fix yourself an advantage, Ben? If you imagine for one moment that I'm going to fall into your arms just because you've got rid of Owen to-night, you're *so* mistaken.'

'Isn't that assumption just a touch conceited?' he said coldly. 'However fatal you imagine your fascination to be, I'd hardly go to the lengths of inducing a miscarriage for Glenys, would I?'

'Oh!' Sophie's bubble of irritation burst instantly. 'She hasn't lost the baby, has she?'

'No, they know now that she'll be OK if she stays quiet. She's in hospital and they've stabilised her condition, but of course Owen has to be there. He wanted to speak to you to give his apologies personally, and to wish you luck. Good of him, under the circumstances, I thought, to find time for that.'

Sophie flashed him a quick, shamefaced look. 'All right. I'm sorry.' Then, with more feeling, 'And I hope to goodness everything's all right for them.'

Ben's attitude towards her didn't soften. 'And now that you've checked my explanation, what's yours for this afternoon?'

'I'll tell you everything that's happened—but later. Please, Ben . . . I've got to get ready now.' She edged towards the door.

'The obvious implication is that you need time to think something up. Forget it, then. As you say, we'd better concentrate on the reason we're here.' He walked towards the bathroom, tugging his tie loose.

'You stupid, suspicious idiot!' Sophie flared as she slammed the door behind herself.

She must not let this wind her up. She had enough to do tonight without coping with an out-of-control temper.

The bath revived her a little, and the bottle of champagne she found in the fridge and opened with a terrible sense of extravagance to be drinking it alone did a lot for the encouragement of bright eyes and delicately flushed skin.

Sophie checked her reflection from all angles. Her hair was up, largely so that the wig would go on easily, but it suited her that way in any case. Her dress was jade green silk, slim-fitting and strapless and cut with French cunning. It was perfectly plain from the front, but at the back a cleverly structured bow at the waist changed into a flounced ruffle that tapered gradually down the centre back to almost nothing at the hem. It was elegant, and it was pert—just her sort of dress. Her small build couldn't take voluminous skirts and ballooning sleeves.

'For half an hour's work, that's not bad,' she told herself as she fixed the glittering diamanté earrings Margo had once given her just as Ben knocked at the door.

Her heart gave a little clench and race as she saw him standing there in his white dinner jacket and remembered the last time he had worn it. He had looked at her in a very different way, then.

'Ready?' he said now, his voice impersonal.

Sophie picked up her black satin embroidered jacket with an offhand 'Yes'. If he didn't want to comment on her appearance, then let him sulk! She had eyes, and she knew what she had seen in the mirror. She walked briskly ahead of him to the lift.

Once they were mingling with the crowd at Pinkerton's the atmosphere between them was sufficiently diluted by the effervescent talk of their table companions to pass unnoticed. Ben chatted with easy charm to Caroline on his left and to the shrewd, smart press women who shared their circular table. With Sophie he made conversation. The others wouldn't know it, but she did, and she made conversation back at him brightly, not betraying how much she would have liked to plaster her avocado Miramar down his pristine shirt front.

Caroline left to go behind the scenes at the Bombe Ananas stage, and Sophie made her own excuses when coffee was served.

'Surely you did it all earlier on?' Ben remarked smoothly, his mouth smiling but his eyes cold.

'There's always something left to see to. You'd be surprised,' she said sweetly.

He would too, she thought as she tore off her jade dress and turned herself rapidly into the Chica Girl. From a vantage point she could see how well the show was going down. Adrenalin swept away her resentment of Ben's attitude, and by the time her own part was reached, Sophie's one concern was to interpret the spirit of the range so that the climax was everything they hoped it would be. Chica was her baby, and it was exciting to be in at the birth in this involved way.

The audience's murmur as she emerged from the box, and their stir and ripple of comment as the fresh, tantalising scent of the Chica perfume flooded the room, was a more subtle music than the group's romantic backing.

Sophie saw nothing of the sea of faces while she was performing. She was the essential girl on the edge of womanhood, discovering her own allure and shyly exploiting and delighting in it, full of dreams and mystery and innocent seduction. Once she left the stage there was no time for retrospection. By the time Caroline was making her witty, sophisticated speech of acknowledgement, Sophie was tearing off the clothes and wig and mask and re-creating her public self.

A member of staff told her that Monsieur Martin was there before she was fully ready, and she stepped out into the corridor to give him the wig in its box with her own hair escaping from its moorings and sliding down in a fall of gold.

Impulsively she leaned forward and kissed the young French *perruquier*, who received the kiss with delight.

'I don't know how we should have managed without your co-operation!' she told him.

'*Mon plaisir*—and my other client's pain if she had seen you in the beautiful hair that does so little for her in comparison!' He lifted her hand to his lips with both of his and lingered over it with all his Gallic charm in full flow.

As he turned to leave by the back street exit, Sophie saw with a plummeting heart that Ben was standing at the other end of the corridor like the personification of doom, reading all the wrong things into what he had just witnessed. In his present mood, he had obviously seen it as amorous, furtive fumblings in the semi-darkness, the kind that leave a girl with her hair tousled and her dress not quite zipped up.

It can't possibly get any worse, Sophie thought recklessly as she said, 'Don't tell me, Ben! You've come to say you liked the show and to give me a pat on the back.'

His eyes swept icily over her bare shoulders and cascading hair.

'That was the original idea, but you appear to have had a surfeit of that sort of thing—on the back, and elsewhere.'

'What's got into you?' she asked him angrily. 'This isn't like you at all. You seem to want to put the worst possible interpretation on everything I do!'

'Are you telling me that he wasn't the man you were with when you should have been back at the hotel, meeting me? He fits the description.'

'He was the man I saw earlier, yes. But each time there was a good reason. Do you want to hear it as I promised, or would it spoil your preconceived ideas?'

Someone was coming along the corridor. Ben stepped closer, his voice low but no less vicious. 'There's no point in talking here. There are people out there waiting to speak to you. I suggest you get back as quickly as possible—after you've removed the traces of what looks like someone's ardent seal of approval plastered all over you.'

Before she could answer he had turned and was striding away. Angry weariness flooded through Sophie. The two days had been exhausting enough and tonight the wig had made her head ache, but what really drained her now was this awful anticlimax. She had been doing everything in her power to promote Chica and protect Country Connection, and every action of hers had been totally misinterpreted.

She went back into the changing-room and did her hair again, stinging with hurt, then switched on a false brightness and returned to the party.

Caroline seemed to grow more lively as the last hours dragged by, but Sophie couldn't think how she was going to remain upright and coherent. Her last shred of energy went into avoiding Ben. There was no shortage of men eager to dance with her, and she managed to get herself swept away each time there seemed danger of Ben coming too close.

At midnight she could take no more and slipped away to get her things and have a taxi called to take her back to the hotel, but Ben appeared from nowhere to grip her arm and stop her.

'Where are you going?' he demanded peremptorily.

'To bed. I've a splitting headache and I've had enough. Nobody really wants to know any more about clothes and perfume now. They're just enjoying themselves.'

His eyes studied her face and he must have seen that she was determined.

'In that case I shall take you, of course. You're not going alone at this hour.'

Sophie was too exhausted to argue. As they drove through town she saw the street lamps flash by in a daze of tiredness, and she walked back into the hotel beside Ben like a sleepwalker.

'Here, give me your key,' he said at the door of her room.

One last stubborn ounce of strength came to her aid. 'I don't need you to open the door,' she said childishly, and fumbled the key into the lock.

The chambermaid must have opened the window to air the room. The through draught flung the door back against the frame and nipped Sophie's finger. It was the last straw.

'Look what you've made me do now!' she burst out in childish outrage, holding up the tip of her finger on which a bead of blood was forming. Suddenly all her resentment of Ben's attitude found tongue. 'I've worked like nobody's business the last two days, Ben Ross!' she said furiously. 'And what thanks do I get from you? Sweet nothing! Well, you can listen now. The Chica Girl broke her ankle this morning and I spent hours haring round London to find that long black hair I was wearing in the show. Yes, *me*. Because there was nobody else, and I had to make myself unrecognisable or you'd have been even more obnoxious. The man you practically accused me of behaving like a whore with was the *wigmaker*, and he risked a lot letting us borrow it, and I was grateful. And when I'd danced and pratted around and done my level best, the last thing I wanted was more insults from you!' She was getting completely out of control, and she didn't care. 'And you never told me I looked nice— but now, oh yes!—you'll be sure to tell me how ghastly I look, and I know I do. And you never danced with me once—never even tried to—but you did with every other lousy woman in the room . . . and now I've got blood on your shirt and you'll blame me for that. And I *never* cry and shout like this. Never!'

Hiccuping and coughing with tears of rage, Sophie had been almost unaware that Ben had drawn her into her room and closed the door, but now she thought that it was just as well or the whole corridor would have been turning out to enjoy the spectacle.

Instead of trying to answer her tirade, he put his hands on her bare shoulders, gently and lovingly, and by the light of the street lamp that was shining palely in through the window she saw that he was looking down into her blotchy, tearstained face with such kindness that she felt herself almost melting in the warmth of it.

Then he said, 'Oh, Sophie!' and there was such a wealth of tenderness in his deep voice that she let her head rest against his blood-stained shirt and slid her arms around him under his dinner jacket, and admitted to herself at last as his own arms folded her close that she had been wanting to do just this for a long, long time.

CHAPTER NINE

BEN had bathed her finger and found a plaster in the bathroom cabinet, and it really was nothing at all to trigger off such an outburst, but Sophie was so glad that it had. Her tears seemed to have flooded out all her doubts and she was left with a warm certainty inside her that was a wonderful feeling to have.

They made tea with the hotel's equipment in the bedroom, then they talked and talked, with Sophie curled up against Ben on the comfortable, squashy settee and just one lamp lit so that the edges of the big room fell away into darkness.

Sophie's mind went back to an earlier part of the day that had been so awful but had ended so beautifully.

'Ben . . .' she said, 'why were you so very cross when we met this evening? I've been pretty awful with you all along, but you've been so patient that I've wanted to scream sometimes!'

She reached up to kiss away any possible bad effect of her words, and it was some time before he said, 'Do you want an answer to that question or not?' and she told him that she did, but being distracted was so very enjoyable.

'Well, it was Glenys and Owen, strangely enough,' he explained. 'I know the threat of losing a child is the very last thing to make you envious of someone, but it was the way Owen reacted. I was in his office when Glenys called him from the hospital, so I couldn't help hearing how they talked to each other. I found myself thinking, That's what I want—that closeness that makes everything bearable as long as the one person you love is there with you. Do you understand that sort of cockeyed thinking?'

Sophie kissed the inside of his wrist and said, 'Yes, I do, and it isn't cockeyed.'

'All the way up the M4 I was going over the way we'd been with each other, the way we'd wasted time, conducted a sort of surface relationship without ever getting through that surface to the real feelings below. I'd thought you needed patience, but I realised when I really thought it through that I hadn't done a very serious job of trying to convince you. I hadn't even told you I loved you—just skirted round it being patronising about your realising the error of your ways, as though you were some kind of fruit that would ripen and drop off into my hand eventually.'

'Which I seem to have done,' smiled Sophie, her lips against his palm.

'I was going to tell you the minute I saw you when I arrived today—yesterday now, I suppose— tell you how even when we first met in Edwards' office and I'd made my up mind in advance that you didn't care tuppence about Charles, just wanted his money—even then I knew that you were the girl I'd end up wanting to spend my life with.'

'You concealed it well!' Sophie glanced mischievously up at him.

'That was because I was trying to convince myself at that point that it was just physical attraction.'

Ben ran his hand slowly down her neck and over her shoulder, then across the soft swell of her breasts. 'And you are very, very lovely, my sweet Sophie...' His voice had deepened, and there was another heady pause that left Sophie in no doubt that he meant what he said, and that the fire of her own response ran equally through every bit of her.

'*Just* physical attraction?' she said breathlessly. 'You mean there's more than this?'

'Much more. I liked the tough way you jumped at the chance to keep Country Connection going instead of wanting your share of its value. And even while you were thinking up schemes that irritated me at first, and that I knew would lead to trouble as well as profit, I loved you for doing it and having the guts to stick to what you believed in.'

'Did you love me at the board meeting?'

'I must have done, or I couldn't have been so incredibly angry that you'd kept your background so secret and then only told me in front of a bunch of other people. I should have known first. I wanted to know everything about you.'

Sophie was quiet and still for a moment, remembering that there was still a vital part of her background that she must tell Ben. Should she do it now? She stirred restlessly, feeling a strong, selfish urge to keep the moment for the two of them...not bring Charles into it just yet.

'So why were you cross?' she reminded him, catching his hand that was running a strand of her hair through his fingers.

'Because I'd got myself so keyed up and convinced that it only needed the right words to get through to you. It seemed so blazingly obvious.

When you weren't there, and that loquacious receptionist gave me such a graphic description of the good-looking Frenchman you'd gone off with, and then handed me that cryptic note that said nothing except that you'd far better things to do than wait for me... I felt the strongest urge to kill that I've ever experienced. You got the sour residue of it.'

'And isn't it odd,' Sophie mused, 'having you behave as though you hated the sight of me made me aware of how much you mattered. I meant it when I said I never cried. I can't remember letting go like that since I was a little girl and a stepfather I was really fond of was given the push by Margo.'

'You should let your feelings run away with you more often.' Ben kissed the tip of her nose. 'Too much control is bad for anyone. I can't see another night like this happening, for instance—the two of us together in a bedroom spending all our time talking!'

Sophie laughed. She couldn't imagine it either, but the talking had been lovely. 'I was so absolutely exhausted, yet now I feel I could stay awake for ever. What time is it, Ben?'

He removed his arm to look at his watch. 'Half past five. The first papers will be out soon.'

'Chica!' Sophie sat up suddenly. She had actually not thought once all night about the launch that had seemed so important over the past weeks— only about Ben and herself. But the write-ups might be in today's editions, and it *did* matter. 'Are you going out to get the papers?'

'Yes, of course. But I want a promise first.'

She looked up at him. 'I thought we'd been more or less making promises all night.'

'More or less won't do.' He pulled her to her feet, keeping her hands in his and holding them against his chest so that she was close to him. 'Tonight's been such an unbelievable time-warp kind of thing. You've got to convince me that you're not going to go back into your *"noli me tangere"* shell as soon as the sun's up.'

Sophie slid her hands up his chest. 'I won't—I know I won't. I'm different now. I don't know why, but I am.' Her hands crept round his neck and she pulled his face down so that she could kiss him and feel again how deliciously familiar his lips were to her now. 'I want you to love me, isn't it obvious?' she said softly against his mouth.

Ben held her away so that he could look into her eyes.

'I'm talking about marriage, Sophie.' The words that could have frightened her a short time ago now made her feel so very happy. It was as though she were just a little drunk, the stage when everything is deliriously witty and wonderful.

'And I thought we were only talking about improper suggestions!' she smiled.

He shook her shoulders. 'Say you're going to marry me! Answer me, woman!'

'Of course I'm going to marry you—man!' she said with shining eyes. Then, the elation of this near-intoxication still running through her veins, 'Only first we've got to read the papers.'

Ben swept her against him with one hand and with the other smacked her bottom. 'You, young lady, are as high as a kite—and so tired without knowing it that you're going to go out like a light any minute now.'

'Not until I've seen the papers,' she said. 'Now *you* promise that you won't look at them until you're back in this room.'

When Ben left, Sophie drew back the curtains and leaned out of the window to watch him going along the road in the early morning light, still wearing his white dinner jacket and striding out with that long, loose stride of his. She didn't call down to him, but he sensed she was watching and looked up, and as he smiled and raised a hand she thought, 'I could die happy at this moment,' then told herself that that was defeatist. She was going to live a lot longer and be, incredibly, even happier.

She took off her poor crumpled green silk dress and put on her dressing gown over her underwear, then sat down to wait.

Ben wasn't long. They divided the half-dozen papers he came back with between them and there was a rapid turning of crackling pages. There were reports on the fashion pages of two of them, both with good photographs. One paper had the girls by themselves, and the other had the girls surrounding Sophie when she first emerged as the Chica Girl. Both gave the range good write-ups, and predicted a good commercial future for both clothes and perfume.

'Is that good, two out of six?' asked Sophie, yawning. Ben had been right about the 'out like a light' business. The print kept dancing before her eyes.

'Two of the biggest circulation dailies? I'll say it is! And there'll be more in the magazines. The agency Caroline uses will look out for those. Yes, you've got Chica off to a very good start, partner.' He looked at Sophie's face, smudgy with tiredness now. 'It looks to me as though the Chica Girl could do with a few hours' sleep.'

'I think you're right.' She yawned again.

'Into bed, then.'

Sophie's eyes flew open at that, and he grinned. 'You—not us. Not yet.'

Half an hour ago she might have been tempted to contradict, but now she was so deliciously, happily sleepy. She climbed into bed, dressing gown and all, and Ben pulled the clothes up and leaned over to kiss her, not goodnight, because it was morning.

'I knew it was you, you know.'

'Knew what?' she said sleepily.

'Knew that you were the Chica Girl.'

'I don't believe you!' Her eyes had flown open again, big and accusing. 'Even Caroline didn't know me when I first put that lot on, and she's known me for years.'

'Caroline hasn't spent as much time coveting various bits of your anatomy as I have. You only had to move and I knew it was you. That's why I hated your wigmaker so much when I saw him with you in the corridor. I thought he'd been watching you . . . and that you'd had the same effect on him as you had on me, only he'd managed to tell you about it before I got the chance.' He kissed her eyes shut again. 'Go to sleep now. I'll see that you're not disturbed until twelve, then we're going to have lunch together and talk about rings and things. Dream about it.'

Sophie clung to him for a moment. 'I wish...'

'So do I. But it wouldn't be wise. Go to sleep now, love.'

She gave in and let the warm drowsiness fill her mind. Almost as soon as the door closed, she slept.

When she awoke she lay still for a moment, testing her feelings, then threw her arms back over her head in a triumphant stretch. It was true. She still felt happier than she had ever been in her whole life. It hadn't changed overnight—not at all.

It was eleven-thirty, and she was seeing Ben at twelve, but she had to speak to him now. She rolled over and picked up the phone, asking to be put through to his room.

'Sophie?' he said immediately.

'How did you know it was me?'

'Just did. I was about to ring you, anyway. Did you sleep well? You haven't changed into a pumpkin overnight?'

She laughed. 'I haven't changed at all—full stop! I'm still me, *your* me, and hardly able to believe it.'

'That's all right, then.' She could hear the smile in his voice. 'In a couple of hours, when we've eaten, we'll see about something tangible to keep reminding you. Are you hungry?'

'Ravenous! Is that too unromantic for words?'

'I like a girl with a healthy appetite.' Ben's voice lowered. 'Healthy *appetites*, actually, come to that.'

'That sounds like the voice of experience.'

'Whatever the voice, I haven't wanted to marry anyone but you—ever.'

Sophie smiled into the phone, realised she was doing it, and didn't care. 'To quote you—"That's all right, then." See you at twelve.'

When she had showered she had a strong urge to tell Caroline, and to have a quick 'exult' about the press reports.

'She's not in today, Miss Pryor,' Caroline's secretary told her. 'She's taking the day off. And actually, she said that anyone who phoned before mid-afternoon would be fired. I think she planned on sleeping the clock round.'

So it would have to be later on in the day, but that didn't matter because by then there would be even more to tell Caro and let her crow about.

It was a lovely October day with a brilliant blue sky and warm sunshine, and by happy coincidence the cashmere sweater and skirt Sophie had with her were sunshine colours—primrose and white.

'I'm glad you're not the kind who overdoes the lipstick,' Ben told her when he had kissed her very thoroughly indeed.

'A dangerous practice—it leaves too much evidence around,' said Sophie.

'Now who sounds experienced?'

'No harm in sounding it, is there?'

They walked down to the restaurant, teasing each other, and Sophie saw a girl sitting by herself at a table watching with a faintly envious look as Ben saw her comfortably seated. I could have been that girl, she thought...sitting alone, on the outside looking in. But now everything's changed.

They ordered crab soufflés to be followed by roast duck, and while they were waiting for the soufflés to be prepared, Sophie said,

'There's so much I want to know about you. Little things, like what you like and don't like to eat . . . and big things—all the things that have happened in your life before I came along.'

Ben smiled. 'We've got a whole lot of talking to do, and a lot of time to do it in.'

Sophie had been telling herself as she got ready that there could be no more holding back on the subject of Charles after today. She still felt an odd reluctance to talk about him, maybe because the subject was so close to her. And yet that was silly, because nothing and no one could be closer than Ben was going to be. She took a big breath.

'Ben . . . There's rather a big thing that I want to tell you.'

He had picked up her left hand and he was playing with her ring finger. 'We'll tell it all, both of us, I promise you. But let's do the important thing first and talk about what sort of ring you'd like.'

Sophie weakly allowed herself to be diverted. 'I really don't have any ideas . . . It's something I've never thought about. It's what it stands for that matters, isn't it?' Suddenly, family being very much in mind, an idea occurred to her. 'I'll tell you what, though, Ben—if there were a family ring, then I'd like that more than anything. Family's something I've never had enough of. I'd like to think of myself as part of a chain with you, with a lot of past and a lot of future.'

Ben was looking at her, his eyes thoughtful.

'A family ring . . . Would you really like that? I don't know.' His finger and thumb stroked up and down her ring finger as though he were imagining the ring in place. 'There is a ring of my mother's, actually. And it could be ideal with your colouring too. It's an emerald, square-cut with diamonds on each side. You've got a lot of green in your eyes, do you know? It showed up very much against that dress you wore last night.'

'It sounds lovely, and yet you sound uncertain. Why, Ben?'

'I suppose because it was the symbol of a very short-lived marriage.' His mouth twisted wryly as she looked at him with disbelief. 'Oh, yes, Sophie, you didn't corner the market in family life that didn't quite work out. But in this case there was no lack of caring, no promiscuity. Just a hopeless sense of failure.'

He paused as the waiter hovered with the soufflés and the wine waiter filled two glasses with iced champagne. When the flurry of activity was over, he raised his glass. 'All that's long over. Here's to the two people who really matter, after all—you and me.'

Sophie drank too, then said, 'You've never talked about your family before. I wondered why.'

Ben put his glass down. 'That wasn't the only reason. I'd better come absolutely clean now while we're on the subject and tell you my dark secret. Don't look so alarmed—it isn't anything too dark! But how about starting on these soufflés before they collapse on us?'

Sophie bent her head and broke into the light golden crust. 'Mmm! This is delicious. But you must go on, Ben. You simply can't tantalise me like that and then clam up on me.'

'Two seconds—this is like eating air, after all.' Perhaps it was twenty seconds before he put his fork down. 'All right. As far as the ring's concerned, I just felt it would be nicer, if you had a family ring, for it to be one with a hundred per cent success record. There's no big secret about that. The main thing I must own up about is my name. You're not going to be Mrs Ross, I'm afraid. Ross is only my middle name, but it's the one I've used professionally, for a special reason.'

Sophie's fork hovered over her plate while she absorbed that.

'Well—' she said after reflection, 'it didn't matter to Juliet, so I don't suppose it does to me, much.'

'You mean: "So Romeo would, were he not Romeo called——"

'"Retain that dear perfection which he owes Without that title..."' Sophie completed. 'Yes, but what is your official name, then, Ben?'

He was watching her closely, waiting for her reaction. 'It's Curtis.'

And well he might expect a reaction, with a coincidence like that!

'That's incredible! You mean like Charles?' she queried.

'Not like Charles. That's the dark secret, Sophie. My name is *his* name. My mother and your uncle were married.'

He was going on speaking because she could see his lips moving, but Sophie felt she had dropped off the edge of the universe into the pit of hell. She struggled to swallow the piece of bread she had been absentmindedly crumbling, but the muscles of her throat were as unable to cope with it as her mind was to accept the frightful thing Ben had so casually and unknowingly revealed.

It's not true, it can't be true! every nerve in her was crying out. But he had said it, quite clearly, and a dreadful coldness at the centre of her was spreading outwards, would go on spreading until she was paralysed with the truth of it.

A sound broke through her whirling darkness.

'... all right, Sophie?' Ben's voice, the voice that had so lightly opened up this chasm between them, came as though from miles away. 'What's the matter? You look like a ghost. What is it?'

She couldn't say it. As long as she didn't take out and speak the knowledge and see his own face reflect the horror she felt, it would go on being not quite real. She made a mammoth effort to swallow, and Ben saw her struggling.

'Is it the crab? Was something wrong with it?'

Sophie seized on the excuse. Anything to get her away—give her time to find the explanation of this awful mistake, because it had to be a mistake, hadn't it? Fate couldn't have led her, mocking and sniggering in anticipation, through all the weeks and months of hostility to this total capitulation only to slam down an iron curtain of unspeakable taboo.

She picked up her napkin and held it to her mouth because it was something for the terror that must be written on her face to hide behind.

'This happens every time,' she said faintly. 'Seafood... I can't take it, but I love it and I keep trying. I've got to go—I'm sorry.'

Ben had half risen, his face concerned. 'I'll come with you.'

'No!' Sophie's voice had been stifled but now it was too sharp, too emphatic. 'No...' she repeated, more apologetically. 'I can't bear anyone around when I'm sick. Give me half an hour. Say I'm sorry—I *am* sorry.' She threw down her napkin and half ran, half stumbled from the restaurant.

'Hello!' said the talkative receptionist. 'That was quick! You've only just gone in.'

Sophie hoped she smiled, because she couldn't speak. It seemed like hours since she had gone in with... since she had gone into the restaurant. His name... she panicked. She couldn't bear even to *think* his name.

The lift wasn't there, so she ran up the two flights to her bedroom. Margo. She had to speak to her. There had always been lies and deceptions with Margo, but this had got to be the biggest lie of all. Margo had deceived Charles as she had deceived so many others. Oh, God, let that be it.

Sophie fumbled through the pages of her address book to find Margo's latest number. She'd got to be there. She had to be. And she had to say what Sophie was desperate to hear, because if she didn't, there would be no point in living.

As the phone rang, she controlled her ragged breathing by a superhuman effort. Be there, Margo, her mind was willing. Answer me!

'Who is it?' The vaguely petulant voice was music. But the right music?

'It's Sophie.'

'Hi, stranger. How've you been doing?'

'Listen, Margo, I want the truth. The absolute truth.'

'What *is* this?' Margo was half laughing, not taking it seriously. 'Some extramural court session? What's my offence this time?'

'This isn't a joke, Margo.' Sophie's fingers gripped the receiver so tightly that it hurt. 'What you told me about Charles... Was it true? Was it?'

Margo's voice cooled. 'That again! We went into all of it, Sophie. I'm not hashing it over again.'

'Please—tell me if you were speaking the truth. Was—was Charles really my father?' She couldn't stop trembling.

'I told you he was,' Margo said shortly.

'But you've told me other things that weren't true. You know you have.'

'Look, Sophie——' Margo sighed impatiently, 'this is both boring and unnecessary.'

'If you told him that so that you could get the money and it wasn't really true...I *must* know!'

'I wanted the money all right. But it was him. I wasn't going to waste my most saleable asset on any old loser, was I? Have I ever?' She must have heard Sophie's strangled half-moan, because her voice suddenly lost its blasé annoyance. 'What *is* the matter, Sophie? Why are you asking all these questions again now? You sound odd.'

Odd...was that how she sounded? Not utterly destroyed...just odd.

'Well, come on! Communicate,' the uncomprehending voice babbled on. 'How are you getting on with——'

Sophie put down the receiver before the question could be completed. For a moment she stood, feeling herself in a vacuum, unable to reach out to anyone. Margo had been the only hope. Now nobody could help her. This was something only she could find her lonely way through.

Soon he . . . No, that was stupid, and stupid was something she couldn't afford to be. Soon Ben would be coming to find out how she was, and she couldn't possibly find the calm and control to do to him what his innocent words had done to her. She must throw her things into the case and go. But where? And if she took a case, she was going to have to stop at the desk and explain or settle the account and Ben might see her there.

Sophie crammed her toilet things into their holdall and pushed it into her shoulder bag, then hurried out into the corridor with her mind still dazedly wondering where she was going. Not back to Carreg Plas. That would be the first place she would be sought. Another thought battered its way into her mind. How could she ever go back to the factory now? And yet if she didn't, she would be dealing a double blow to Ben because she would be breaking the terms of the will and the business would be sold.

The lift was coming up, and she looked round frantically, realising that there was no way of knowing if Ben would be in it. A bathroom door was open, and she slipped inside. She didn't look as footsteps strode along the corridor. She knew with that sixth sense that was going to torture her until she had rid herself of the past that it was Ben.

She held her breath, and went on holding it until she was down the stairs and out in the road, running to the taxi that by some miracle had just dropped a fare.

It was only as she got in that she knew where she was going—to Caroline, the one who had always been a refuge and wouldn't hesitate to give her shelter now until she could cope with this situation that all her instincts still fought to disbelieve.

Caroline lived in Hampstead in a flat in a converted big old house overlooking the Heath. There was a breeze blowing in contrast to the dusty closeness of central London, and Sophie stood pressing the bell with her eyes closed, wishing it could blow her away into nothingness.

When Caroline opened the door, still in her dressing gown, Sophie just said,

'I need help.' The last remaining remnant of initiative that had got her here was fading rapidly, and she felt to be sinking into deathly apathy.

Caroline saw what was written on the pale face and in the look in Sophie's eyes.

'You've got it, love,' she said, and drew Sophie inside.

CHAPTER TEN

CAROLINE poured a stiff brandy and soda and stood over Sophie while she drank every drop of it, then she fetched a thick cardigan because Sophie was shivering although it was still warm and sunny. After that she sat down and said calmly, 'All right. Start talking if you can.'

She sat and listened, strangely quiet and subdued for her, while Sophie gradually stumbled through her story in disjointed sentences. Her story...Ben's story...hers and Ben's...the latter a story that had hardly started and now could never finish.

'So that's it,' she concluded, drained by the effort of putting it all into words. The act of making it all real by speaking it had been indescribably painful. 'I was so horrified, Caro, so speechless with the irony of it, that I couldn't have spoken to Ben, not right away. How on earth am I going to tell him?'

'He's still at the hotel, I take it?'

'I suppose so... wondering where on earth I am. I didn't leave a note or anything. All my things are still in the room.'

Caroline was looking at her, her eyes full of sympathy.

'You've got to talk to him, you know.'

'I do know—but I had to have a breathing space.' Her eyes seemed shades darker than normal as she looked at Caroline. 'It isn't the sort of thing you can find instant acceptance for.' Her voice shook.

'I don't know whether I can find it in me to accept it at all.'

'What else can you do, if it's true? Do you believe it?'

'I don't want to...desperately don't want to. I've spoken to Margo—it was the first thing I did when I got up to my room. But she was adamant about Charles, and I practically begged her to say otherwise. So I've got to believe it, haven't I?'

'What about Ben?'

'You mean, do I believe him? Why else would he say what he did? And there are so many other things that make sense now. His looking after Charles when he was ill, for instance...that always seemed more than the average kindness of one working colleague to another. And before that, the fact that he gave up work at a prestigious firm in Switzerland to come and bury himself in a place that wasn't going to make any international waves. Why would he do that without a strong personal reason? Then there was Charles leaving him half the factory, making us both equal...It all adds up, doesn't it?' Sophie crumpled up, hiding her face in the wing of the chair. 'Oh, if only there hadn't been all this damned secrecy! If only we'd known where we stood right from the start.'

'Poor old Sofe...' said Caroline gently, the old nickname rising to the surface of her mind on the sadness that was thickening her voice. 'Your life never was without its complications, but the devil himself must have cooked up this one for you.' She straightened her back and ran her fingers through her copper hair. Circumstances were never allowed to get the better of Caroline. 'Well, it's there, isn't it? And we've got to do something about it. The first thing, I presume, is to let Ben know where you are. Do you want me to ring the hotel?'

'I'll do it. I can't lean on you for everything. I'll tell him I'll be back in a couple of hours. Not tell him, leave a message for him.'

'He must be either worried to death or blazing mad.'

'Either of which is preferable to the way he's going to feel when I've talked to him, isn't it?'

This was so patently true that Caroline could find nothing to say in reply. She got up. 'I'm going to sling some clothes on, and then I'm going to make you some toast, since you walked out on lunch.'

Sophie shuddered. 'I couldn't eat a thing.'

'Yes, you could. Only a bit of toast, Sophie, not a three-course meal. You're going to have to make yourself do everything that's normal until you gradually begin to feel normal again. And you will, Sophie. This has been the most ghastly, vile shock for you, but I've seen you weather storms before.'

Sophie's eyes looked miserably at her. 'Never one like this.'

Caroline took her hand and pulled her to her feet. 'Go and make that phone call.'

Ben had been turning the hotel upside down for her—even talking about contacting the police, the receptionist said before Sophie had the chance to relay her message.

'Tell him——' She looked at her watch. It was still only a quarter to two, although time seemed to have stood still. 'Tell him I'll be back no later than four.' Two hours, two years—would she ever be ready to tell him? Sophie thought as she put down the phone.

'I'm in the kitchen!' called Caroline.

Sophie went through and sat on a stool at the white-topped surface. Caroline had changed into jeans and a red sweater that killed the colour of her copper hair—a sign that she was not as calm as she was trying to be. She put a plate with a slice of toast and a mug of steaming coffee in front of Sophie, and Sophie thought the smell of both would make her sick, but she forced herself to try and do something with them for Caroline's sake. Topaz, Caroline's marmalade tabby, curled up in her basket on the central heating boiler, raised a head and inspected Sophie, then tucked her nose back into her tail again.

'Now——' said Caroline, sitting on the next stool and propping her chin on her hands, 'I've been thinking. We've no option but to assume Margo's telling the truth—there's no way of checking up on her story, is there? But what Ben said... it sounds as though there ought to be public records that can be checked.'

'Ben isn't the sort to lie. Why should he?'

'I'm just trying to explore every avenue. Suppose Ben had been given as garbled a version of the truth as you were? It's an extreme chance, I know, but it is one.'

'It's only putting off the agony,' Sophie said dully. 'What's the point?'

'Putting off accepting painful facts until they're proved beyond any doubt is what you should always do. Ben did say "marriage" specifically, didn't he?'

'Yes.'

'Then it's got to be registered—and his birth too, presumably. Sophie, I'm going to check those two facts. I want you to suspend everything. Belief, disbelief... every single feeling, until I've done that.'

Sophie pushed the plate away and buried her face in her hands.

'That won't be difficult. I feel totally numb. Nothing seems real.'

'Don't try to make it so. Just exist for an hour. I'll take a taxi both ways so that I don't have to try and park.'

Caroline shepherded Sophie into the sitting-room and settled her in a chair overlooking the walled garden, then darted into the kitchen again and came back to dump Topaz on Sophie's lap.

'Stroke her. She's a very comforting cat.'

Topaz turned round two or three times and then slumped against Sophie's chest, a rumbling purr starting up.

'You come up with the most extraordinary solutions to things,' Sophie sighed, but her hand began automatically moving from nose to tail over the cat's silky fur.

'Just keep on doing it,' ordered Caroline. 'All you have to do is make your mind a blank and stroke the cat. I'll be back as quickly as I can. Don't think any more until then.'

When she had gone, Sophie closed her eyes and let the cat's vibrating purr take over the emptiness in her. It was easy not to think. When you are confronted by the unthinkable, the mind wants nothing more than to reject it.

It couldn't go on like this, of course. If she opened her eyes and looked at her watch she would see its hands moving slowly forward towards the time when she would have to go and talk to Ben…but she wasn't going to open her eyes. Topaz had shuffled up until her head was tucked under

Sophie's chin, soft and warm, and as Caroline had said, strangely comforting.

The phone rang in a little while, and she had to put Topaz down while she went to answer it. Someone wanted Caroline to ring them back about a theatre ticket. Someone bright and jolly-sounding, whose life was probably one uncomplicated round of fun. Sophie left the phone off the hook because the voice had brought the outside world into the flat and she couldn't cope easily with that—not yet.

Topaz had gone back into her basket, and it seemed unfair to keep shunting her around, so Sophie threw the toast, out of which she had only taken one bite, into the bin and emptied the coffee down the sink before washing the dishes. She would eat again, of course, because nobody stays in a state of shock, which was what she supposed she was in now, for ever. But at this moment she felt she would never be normal again. It was as though someone had poured molten glass over her to set and form a shell that cut off sight and sound and feeling. Her hands as she washed the mug and plate felt stiff and unnatural, as paralysed as her brain.

The doorbell shrilled piercingly, and that at least roused some response in her because it would be Caroline, gone without her key because she had been so eager to rush off and help in a situation where no help was possible, and the only thing that could come from her return was confirmation of the truth that Sophie wasn't going to be able to close her mind against any longer.

She went slowly to the door and opened it—and Ben was standing there.

Sophie stepped back with the shock of it, and he strode past her into the flat and through to the sunny sitting-room. Then he turned to face her, and his familiar face was unfamiliar to her because of what she had to tell him, but he didn't wait for her to speak.

'I don't know what the hell you've been playing at,' he said, 'but I do know that your amazing allergy to crab was the biggest bit of play-acting you've ever indulged in—though it had me fooled for long enough to give you the chance to bolt over here. True?'

Sophie moistened her lips and nodded slowly. 'Yes, it's true.' Her voice sounded thin and unlike itself.

'Of course it's true,' he said coldly. 'I remember every little thing you've said or done or looked from the moment we met—which is more than you appear to do. When I took you to the Fox and Grapes for lunch that first working day at Country Connection, you chose—actually chose—seafood flan, and you ate every scrap without the least ill effect.'

Sophie thought for a second how ludicrous it was that they should be talking of food when there was so grave a matter waiting to be dealt with.

'None of that matters,' she said woodenly.

'Doesn't it? And what about this? Does this matter?' He put his hand in the pocket of his suit and threw an envelope down on to the low table between them. 'Another bit of trivia that your good friend Caroline seemed to think needed urgent attention. Your friend seems as good at dramatics as you are. She practically fell over herself to tell me how important it was that I give you this before we talk. She didn't say why, any more than she explained just why she thought it vital that I should come haring over here after you instead of letting you recover your senses and come back to the hotel.'

Sophie stared at the envelope. She could guess what was in it: copies of the certificates—proof she didn't really need—and Caroline was ducking out of the situation. Who could blame her? She'd tried. What more could she do now, apart from allow this privacy for the things that had to be said?

'Sit down, Ben,' she said quietly. 'I've got to talk to you.'

'Why now and not then?' he demanded hotly. 'Isn't there enough trust between us for you to come right out with something that upsets you? Why should the talking be an afterthought and flight come first?'

'What if the talking only leads to something that's too awful to contemplate?' said Sophie.

'*Nothing* is too awful for us to face together.'

He didn't know that what she had to tell him meant the end of their kind of togetherness, and every hurt and angry word he uttered made what she had to do more difficult.

'What was it that scared the sense out of you, Sophie? We were talking family, weren't we? Was it that that stirred up the fears you swore you'd done with? If so, why couldn't you tell me instead of running away?'

Sophie said, 'It was talking about family... but not in the way you think, Ben. Let me try to tell you.' She went over to the window so that her back was towards him and she couldn't see his eyes. She couldn't bear to see what would happen in the depths of them when he knew.

'Go on, then,' he prompted impatiently, and she swallowed hard.

'Margo always told me that my father died before I was born, and I grew up believing that. I even made excuses for the way she went from man to man, telling myself that her first marriage, the one to which I belonged, must have been so perfect that no other relationship could live up to it. Well, that wasn't true. I know now that she didn't love my father at all. She used him, in the most cynical, calculating way possible. She got every penny she could out of him in return for absolutely nothing...quite cold-bloodedly.' Sophie's voice died away into silence as she stared fixedly out at the garden, and Ben said after a moment,

'The fact that Margo is no good and has more than enough to answer for as far as your emotional development is concerned isn't new. You're not telling me anything that explains today specifically.'

Sophie clenched her hands and forced herself to go on.

'I haven't finished yet. Earlier this year I found out that this "wonderful marriage" of my imagination had never existed. I wasn't Adam Curtis's daughter as Margo had always led me to believe— there was no Adam Curtis...and there had been no marriage. I found all this out in a rather shocking way. My true father wrote me a letter...not explaining the full awfulness of what Margo had done—I had to go to her for that—but telling me that all my life he'd been there, and Margo had prevented my knowing him. By the time I got the letter it was too late. He really was dead.'

There was another pause while Sophie tried to steel herself for the last giant step she must take.

'Go on,' Ben said quietly.

She drew in a shuddering breath. 'I got the letter the day I came to Abergavenny to hear the contents of Charles's will—the day I first met you, Ben. Mr Edwards gave it to me.' Her throat was dry and painfully constricted. 'Do I have to say any more? Can't you guess who my father was?'

The air in the room was deathly still. It seemed to Sophie like the stillness of impending storm, the stillness that silences the birds minutes before an earthquake tears the world apart.

She had closed her eyes against the painful brightness and normality of the sun-bathed garden, and at last she heard Ben speak. Only three words, his voice toneless, giving away nothing of his re-action . . . not even questioning, just stating the fact that was going to change their lives.

'You mean Charles.'

She knew the turmoil that must exist beneath his surface calm, and she did the only thing she could to help him.

'Yes, Charles. Just go, Ben. I know what you're feeling. There's nothing either of us can say.'

His reply, when it came after another silence, was so unexpected that Sophie opened her eyes and saw him reflected in the window glass, leaning forward in his chair, his face intent.

'But you're wrong. There's so much to be said. I know exactly what happened now!' He got up and she could see in the glass that he was coming towards her and she couldn't bear that. Perhaps he was strong enough to achieve this instant accept-ance, this instant switch of attitude, but it was going to take so very much longer before she could even think of him without pain. She swung round, her hands raised defensively, her voice strangled as she said,

'Don't Ben. Don't come near me!'

He stopped immediately, his voice compassionate.

'All right. It's all right, Sophie—really it is. Don't look like that. I'm going to explain it all. Only sit down, please, love, before you fall down.' He stepped back and sat on the arm of the chair he had been using, but Sophie stayed where she was, pressed against the warm glass of the window, transfixed like an animal at bay.

'I want you to think back carefully to what I said at lunch,' he went on when he realised that she was not going to move. 'I told you that Charles and my mother were married, didn't I? And the instant you heard that, you switched off? Am I right? You went into your own private hell and didn't hear another word?'

Sophie nodded slowly, as all the pain of that moment threatened to overwhelm her again. She could feel the glassy shell that had been cutting her off from the world beginning to splinter. If Ben went on looking at her so tenderly, it would shatter and fall away and she would be left to face him in all her weakness, and she didn't know how she could bear that.

'Sophie, if you'd gone on listening, if you'd not been too shocked to hear the rest, you'd have heard me say that I was twelve at the time——' He repeated the words emphatically. 'Twelve years old when Charles and my mother married—old enough not to think much of the idea and find it vaguely embarrassing. More than half the age you are now, Sophie.'

She heard the words, but they skated around the surface of her mind and didn't penetrate to her understanding. All the defences she had been struggling to maintain wouldn't let her risk a shred of hope unless she was convinced of its truth.

'But you told me that you had Charles's name.'

'And I do, but not as a birthright. I've told you—I was awkward, truculent, finding fault with everything about the idea, including the fact that my name would be different from my mother's. Charles said that nothing would give him more pleasure than for me to take his name as well. He adopted me. In the years we were together he couldn't do enough for me. His eagerness to please and care was almost like a fever.'

And it *was* a kind of fever, Sophie realised in the light of all she knew. It was Charles trying to make up for the child and the marriage Margo had so adamantly refused him.

Her eyes fell on the envelope from Caroline that Ben had thrown on the table, and suddenly she knew that the proof her mind still craved was there—had been there all the time, only she had thought it the wrong kind of proof.

She picked up the envelope and tore it open...read the copy marriage certificate...Charles Curtis, Bachelor, and Alice Ross, Widow, and the date. Even her shattered mind could do the sum and work out that Ben *was* twelve at the time. And the birth certificate...Benedict James...Mother, Alice, née Archer...Father, Andrew Timothy Ross. *Andrew Timothy Ross.* She had heard the truth, and now she could see it in her hands. She could dare to believe.

There was another scrap of paper torn from a notebook, with Caroline's triumphant scrawl across it: 'You see? And what the hell have you done with my phone?'

In a daze Sophie went across the room to the forgotten telephone and put the receiver back on the hook. Then, right there as she bent over the table, the tide of feeling came flooding back through her, painful as returning circulation to a frozen limb. All the sorrow she had not let herself express and all the joy she could now allow herself warred in her heart and head, and escaped from her lips in a tortured drawn-out 'O-o-o-h!' that was part pain, part indescribable relief.

She heard Ben's voice.

'Sophie,' he said softly, tenderly, 'come to me, love. You can now.'

She could hardly see for tears, but somehow she managed to cross the space that separated them, and then she was in his arms, her face pressed against his, and his arms holding her...just holding her, and that was enough for the first few precious minutes. When it became clear that she still had a lot of healing crying to do, Ben gently lifted her and took her to the chair by the window in the sun, and sat holding her on his knee until the flood of tears was exhausted.

Sophie gave a great, shuddering sigh. 'Oh—and to think I used to consider myself calm and level-headed!'

Ben's arms tightened round her and he kissed the top of her head. She could feel the smile in his voice. 'You will be again, I hope. I don't fancy going through life with a permanently wet shirt! Better now?'

She slid her arms round his neck and snuggled more closely to him.

'Mmmh. Better—and getting better by the second.'

'Ready to talk a bit more now?'

'Yes. I want to know how it all happened.'

'I doubt that we'll ever know everything. Most of it was locked up in poor unhappy Charles's private hell.'

They talked, comparing dates, and gradually a picture of the two years surrounding Sophie's birth began to emerge.

Margo's marriage to Don Pryor and his adoption of Sophie must have ended any lingering hope Charles had of Margo one day turning to him and allowing him to know his child. It was at that time that Ben's mother came to act as housekeeper for him and he saw in her and her son both the chance to do something to help them, and the possibility of something like the family life that he craved, with her son accepting his name.

'I was never told precisely what went wrong,' Ben told her. 'I was away at public school by that time—something that would have been out of the question without Charles's support—but with true adolescent arrogance I was more concerned at the time about whether I would be able to stay on there than about the success or failure of a marriage that had always been in my eyes a vaguely uncomfortable affair. Charles settled enough money on us to see me through, of course, being Charles. Looking back on it now, I can see how it must have been...Charles desperately unhappy because he still loved Margo, quite blindly, unable to be anything but the unsatisfactory shadow of the husband my mother would have wanted. She would have hoped for a real marriage. She was an all or nothing woman.'

'Was?' Sophie asked tentatively.

'Yes. So I'm afraid we're never going to know more from her. She died just before I came back to Wales, otherwise I don't suppose I should ever have joined up with Charles again.'

'Why did you come back?'

'Pure chance, really. I'd lost touch with Charles after university, but he saw a paper of mine in a scientific journal and wrote to me. He'd been told to take it easy, and seeing that I was involved in cosmetic allergy research and our fields linked up, he wrote to ask if I would be interested in taking over from him at Country Connection. Very diffidently, giving me every chance to refuse.'

'But you didn't. What made you accept? It must have seemed very small fry after the Swiss company you were working for.'

'I'd come to the end of my research there, more or less. And I suppose that from my then mature standpoint, I realised that I owed Charles a lot.'

'You didn't use his name, though.'

'For several reasons. I didn't want to be known as some kind of family connection and then find that the work just didn't satisfy me—leaving Charles in the unenviable position of having everyone know that he'd been let down yet again. He appreciated that fact, and he didn't expect me to keep on with work I didn't enjoy. And it was easier for me to familiarise myself with the different phases of the business as a stranger than as some kind of family connection, however remote.'

'You stayed on. Was that out of a sense of duty?'

'No. I was surprisingly happy in Llangellert. The place and the work got quite a hold on me—plus the fact that in that particular area it was so badly needed. I did grow very fond of Charles, though. I think he was happier in those years than in all the rest of his life.'

'I'm glad...'

Ben stroked her hair and they were quiet for a moment, then he said, 'So that's the past dealt with, and I think now we should let it rest. There's one important thing to remember, though.'

'What's that?' Sophie sat up so that she could look into his face.

'The fact that we both come from people who couldn't settle for second-best love.' His eyes held hers. 'For me it will be only you and always you. I want you to know that.'

She looked steadily back at him and knew that no words at their official marriage would be more binding than the ones they spoke now. 'And for me, Ben. Only and always.'

'And there's a sort of justice in the fact that you will at last bear the name Curtis, isn't there?'

'A wonderful justice.' Sophie's eyes shone. '"What's in a name?"'... Shakespeare wasn't always right, was he? Sometimes it can mean so much.'

'But only when it belongs to the right man.'

'Only then.' She sank back against him with the sweetest, most exultant feeling of belonging. 'And then,' she said, 'there truly is a "dear perfection".'

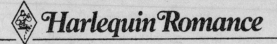

Coming Next Month

2971 REMEMBER, IN JAMAICA Katherine Arthur
For three years Claire has battled with her boss over his violent
temper, impossible dreams and insane schedules. Suddenly,
once she agrees to the working trip in Jamaica, Terrill changes
into a pussycat. Claire can't help feeling suspicious.

2972 NO LOVE IN RETURN Elizabeth Barnes
The only reason Eve has worked as a model is to pay for her
brother's education. To the imperious Jackson Sinclair,
however, *model* is synonymous with *gold digger*. And there
seems to be no way to persuade him he's wrong.

2973 SNOWFIRE Dana James
Beth can't pass up the chance to be official photographer on an
Iceland expedition, though she's stunned to find her estranged
husband, Dr. Allan Bryce, as leader. Even more shocking is the
realization that Allan thinks he was the injured party!

2974 SYMPATHETIC STRANGERS Annabel Murray
Recently widowed Sandra begins to build a new life for herself
and her young twins by helping friends of her mother's in Kent.
Yet when lord of the manor Griff Faversham pursues her, she
refuses to consider marriage to another wealthy man.

2975 BED, BREAKFAST & BEDLAM Marcella Thompson
In helping Bea McNair establish an Ozark Mountain retreat for
Bea's ailing friends, Janet dismisses Lucas McNair's plan to
move his mother to a Little Rock retirement home. There's no
dismissing Lucas, though, when he descends upon her like a
wrathful God.

2976 MOWANA MAGIC Margaret Way
Ally can't deny the attraction between herself and the powerful
Kiall Lancaster, despite his mistrust of her. Common sense tells
her to leave. But first she determines to straighten out Kiall's
chauvinistic attitude. Not an easy task!

Available in April wherever paperback books are sold, or
through Harlequin Reader Service:

In the U.S.
901 Fuhrmann Blvd.
P.O. Box 1397
Buffalo, N.Y. 14240-1397

In Canada
P.O. Box 603
Fort Erie, Ontario
L2A 5X3

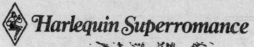

Have You Ever Wondered If You Could Write A Harlequin Novel?

Here's great news—Harlequin is offering a series of cassette tapes to help you do just that. Written by Harlequin editors, these tapes give practical advice on how to make your characters—and your story—come alive. There's a tape for each contemporary romance series Harlequin publishes.

Mail order only

All sales final

TO: *Harlequin Reader Service*
Audiocassette Tape Offer
P.O. Box 1396
Buffalo, NY 14269-1396

I enclose a check/money order payable to HARLEQUIN READER SERVICE® for $9.70 ($8.95 plus 75¢ postage and handling) for EACH tape ordered for the total sum of $_____*
Please send:

☐ Romance and Presents   ☐ Intrigue
☐ American Romance   ☐ Temptation
☐ Superromance   ☐ All five tapes ($38.80 total)

Signature_____
                                                (please print clearly)
Name:_____
Address:_____
State:_____Zip:_____

*Iowa and New York residents add appropriate sales tax.   AUDIO-H